THE IVY OF AN EARL

THE HOLIDAYS OF THE ARISTOCRACY
BOOK 6

LINDA RAE SANDE

ALSO BY LINDA RAE SANDE

The Daughters of the Aristocracy

The Kiss of a Viscount

The Grace of a Duke

The Seduction of an Earl

The Sons of the Aristocracy

Tuesday Nights

The Widowed Countess

My Fair Groom

The Sisters of the Aristocracy

The Story of a Baron

The Passion of a Marquess

The Desire of a Lady

The Brothers of the Aristocracy

The Love of a Rake

The Caress of a Commander

The Epiphany of an Explorer

The Widows of the Aristocracy

The Gossip of an Earl

The Enigma of a Widow

The Secrets of a Viscount

The Widowers of the Aristocracy

The Dream of a Duchess

The Vision of a Viscountess

The Conundrum of a Clerk

The Charity of a Viscount

The Cousins of the Aristocracy

The Promise of a Gentleman

The Pride of a Gentleman

The Holidays of the Aristocracy

The Christmas of a Countess

The Knot of a Knight

The Holiday of a Marquess

The Snow Angel of a Duke

The Ivy of an Earl

The Heirs of the Aristocracy

The Angel of an Astronomer

The Puzzle of a Bastard

The Choice of a Cavalier

The Bargain of a Baroness

The Jewel of an Earl's Heir

The Vixen of a Viscount

The Honor of an Heir

The Rose of a Sultan's Son

The Ladies of the Aristocracy

The Lady of a Grump

The Lady of a Sultan

The Pursuit of a Duchess

The Lords of the Aristocracy

The Abduction of an Earl

Beyond the Aristocracy

The Pleasure of a Pirate

The Making of a Mistress

The Bride of a Baronet

The Caton of a Captain

Puss and Pots

The Betrothal of a Baron

The Grand Tours of the Aristocracy

A Courtship in Catania

Revenge of the Wallflowers

The Wager of a Wallflower

Stella of Akrotiri

Origins

Deminon

Diana

The Lyon's Den (Dragonblade Publishing)

The Courage of a Lyon

The Lady of a Lyon

Note: Translations of select titles are available in German, Italian, Spanish and Portuguese.

CHAPTER 1
A MOST UNEXPECTED ARRIVAL

ecember 1815, near Castleford, Yorkshire

When the butler opened the door of Ritchfield Park, he wasn't expecting Lady Ivy, Countess of Ritchfield, to blow into the vestibule along with a flurry of snowflakes and a biting wind worthy of a North Sea storm. He was so stunned at the sudden arrival of it all, it took him a moment to realize exactly who had crossed over the threshold.

"Oh!" Ivy said, holding her arms out as if she was having trouble keeping her balance. Until the servant managed to shut the door against the winter wind, she kept her face aimed away from the cold.

"My lady?" Graves said in surprise, stepping around to regard her with disbelief. "Is... is that you?"

His uncertainty was due to the layer of white stuff that made her look as if she had been a snowman come to life.

"Yes, yes, it's me," Ivy said, pulling the snow-covered hat from her head to reveal her flame-colored coiffure and reddened cheeks.

The simple act created even more flurries in the vestibule

as the crystals danced about before falling to the floor. Even after she stomped her booted feet, snowflakes still encased her hunter green redingote. For a moment, she looked as if she could have been one of the evergreen trees surrounding the country estate after it had been decorated for the holiday.

"Apologies for not having sent word I'd be coming for Christmas, but I couldn't abide another day in the city," she explained.

"Quite all right, my lady," Graves replied, although he didn't sound convincing.

"I do not envy Walker's duty on this day," she said, referring to the coach driver who was at that very moment seeing to unhitching the four Cleveland Bays that had managed the snowy trip from a coaching inn near Wakefield.

Although the Great North Road out of London had been clear for the first hundred miles or so, snow had begun to fall on their third day of travel. By the time they departed the coaching inn where they had spent the night, the temperature had dropped enough to keep the road from becoming muddy. Conditions worsened, and at the next stop, she had suggested they spend the night there. Walker insisted he could get them to Ritchfield Park before noon, though, and so they had continued.

Ivy had a suspicion she knew why he was so anxious to reach the Ritchfield country estate. Walker had always held a candle for one of the housemaids employed there. She hoped he would be rewarded with a warm bed and a tumble later that night.

"I do hope there's room in the carriage house for the coach?"

Graves stared at her a moment, as if he was uncertain about how to respond. "Uh... I'm sure if there is not, Walker will make room, my lady."

"Oh, and do see to it that Perkins is given something extra

in his pay this month," she continued, unaware of his hesitation. "The poor man is already out there seeing to my trunks. Oh, and I could use some tea when you get to it. It's been an age since I had a decent cup of tea."

Blinking, the butler was about to ask how it was possible Perkins could be seeing to her trunks—he hadn't seen the footman go out—when a pounding sounded at the front door. He gingerly opened it, this time standing in front lest it fly open and allow another snowstorm into the vestibule.

Upon seeing the footman, Graves opened the door wider. The snow still left from Ivy's arrival swirled about and was joined with a new blast from outside.

Perkins wedged himself and the trunk through the opening, scoffing at the butler as the new flurry of snow whirled about. "You want me to freeze out there?" Perkins scolded. "Let me in."

Graves murmured an apology, but his attention went back to the countess as the footman hurried past with the trunk mounted on his shoulder. He winced at seeing the wet tracks left by Perkins as he made his way through the front hall and up the stairs.

Finally aware something wasn't quite right with the butler —he was paler than usual and seemed rather bothered—Ivy regarded him with a curious expression. "Whatever is wrong, Graves? You look as if you've seen a ghost."

The butler swallowed, his gaze going past her to the man who had appeared on the threshold of the study and had been watching them since before Perkins' arrival. "Pardon me, my lady. I'll see to the tea," Graves said, before he hurried off as if shot from a cannon, leaving Ivy displaying a look of confusion.

Whatever was wrong with Graves? Usually a fastidious and efficient servant, he was none of those on this day. He hadn't taken her hat, her redingote, or her gloves.

When Ivy turned around, she immediately understood why the servant had acted as he had.

Garbed in a most fashionable navy topcoat, a scarlet embroidered waistcoat, tan leather breeches, and a pair of black Hobys in which she could probably see her reflection, her husband of nearly thirty years was regarding her with an unreadable expression from where he stood on the threshold of his study.

Ivy was reminded of the very first time she had seen the earl. He was standing much as he was now, an impassive expression making him appear bored while he surveyed the young ladies making their presentations to the queen before the first ball of the season in 1784.

As it was now, his dark hair had been cut unfashionably short, but then he had already inherited the earldom and was required to wear a wig during Parliament. His harsh features did not make him a particularly handsome man. From somewhere in his lineage, Viking marauders and soldiers had contributed an ancient Roman nose, stark cheekbones, and slashes for eyebrows. His eyes, a piercing blue-gray, had pinned her the moment she caught sight of him, and she remembered feeling as if he could see through her gown. His tall physique was that of a fencer, lean but athletic, and time had obviously not changed it.

Nor had it changed the way her own body reacted to seeing him.

Her breath caught in her throat. Her heart had picked up its pace to the point she could hear her pulse pounding in her ears. Her breasts, already larger than most, plumped, and her nipples tightened behind her stays, the fabric chafing the tender skin. The space at the top of her thighs grew damp, and dammit if she could feel her pulse there, too.

Dammit all to hell!

How terribly inconvenient Robert, Earl of Ritchfield, should be at Ritchfield Park the very same time as she!

Well, she would just have to make the best of it. Pretend all was well. Behave in a manner befitting a countess. Be respectful. Attempt an air of friendliness.

Act as if the past ten years hadn't left her feeling bereft and alone.

They might be estranged, only seeing one another on occasion when he was in London for Parliament, but they were not enemies. Nor were they divorced.

Seeing him like this, though—his harsh features softened in the dimmer interior lighting of the country estate—had her inhaling softly. Ivy was reminded of their second meeting in London. At the time, the enigmatic earl had been on the list of every Mayfair mother with a daughter of marriageable age— her own mother included. Although Ivy hadn't found Robert Strathford, Earl of Ritchfield, particularly handsome, her body had reacted in a most unusual manner.

Much as it was still doing now, damnation.

How was it he could so easily have her stomach filling with flutterbies and her body begging for his touch? Her nipples tightening into hard buds and frissons skittering beneath her skin? Without so much as saying or doing anything but standing there? Looking all perfectly clothed and far too calm?

Whatever chill she had felt from the winter weather outside quickly succumbed to the fever she seemed to be suffering on the inside.

Determined to be on her very best behavior, Ivy pulled back her shoulders and made sure she displayed a pleasant expression.

Before she could say or do anything else, though, Robert disappeared into the study and shut the door.

Ivy let out the breath she had been holding in a huff. Deciding she wasn't going to allow his presence to change her plans for the upcoming Christmas holiday, she placed her hat on the shelf, pulled off her gloves, and wriggled out of her redingote. After hanging it on one of the pegs, she wiped her feet and followed Perkins' tracks up the stairs and to her bedchamber.

She was the Countess of Ritchfield, after all, and nothing—not even her husband—was going to ruin Christmas.

CHAPTER 2
AN EARL SCOLDS HIMSELF

Meanwhile, in the study at Ritchfield Park

"Coward," Robert murmured to himself as he leaned against the closed door to his study and banged the back of his head against the hard wood panel. Of all the people who might have paid a call at his country estate in the middle of the worst winter on record in England, the very last person he expected to arrive was his wife.

He was sure she preferred London for Christmas. Or perhaps it was Bath? Certainly not Brighton. He couldn't imagine spending Christmas in Brighton, and most certainly not this year.

Perhaps that's where *he* should have gone instead of making the trek to Ritchfield Park. Even Graves had been surprised to see him upon his arrival the day before, as if he had been a ghost of Christmas past come to haunt him. Given the flurry of snow surrounding his arrival, he probably looked like a ghost.

Not like Ivy had, all covered in snow and looking like an angel, her hair still coppery red and her cheeks rosy from the cold. She might have been wearing rags and she would still have his breath catching as it had the very first time he saw her.

Dressed in a white velvet court gown festooned with satin bows and her red coiffure crowned with a white ostrich feather, she has been accompanied by her mother as she was presented to the queen. The ruffled neckline barely hid her rising moons, and he remembered wondering if those moons might escape the confines of her stomacher when she curtsied.

They hadn't, of course, but the thought of tracing her neckline with a fingertip, the skin so soft and warm, had his index finger twitching even now.

Ivy had always had glorious breasts. Full and fleshy, topped with rosy nipples, they had provided a pillow for his head after they made love and a cushion when he had her pulled against him on cold winter nights. He had never tired of holding them, stroking them, kissing them, or of suckling their engorged nipples.

Although gravity might eventually have its way with them—perhaps it already had—there wasn't another pair on the planet he had adored like hers.

Nor was there anyone else with that particular shade of red hair. The color of flames when under the sun and shades of dark copper when indoors, Ivy's hair shimmered as if it was made of metal. It was soft, though, like silk, and wavy when it wasn't bound into the elaborate coiffures her lady's maid constructed every morning before breakfast and every night before dinner.

At one time, he had enjoyed removing the pins that held up all those waves, plucking them out one after another, silently counting to be sure he found them all. He had made a sort of game of it, careful to remove as many pins as possible without disturbing the coiffure until finding the one pin that would send it all crashing down at once in a mass of coppery waves and curls.

Remembering how she had looked upon her arrival a few minutes ago, he wondered how many pins her lady's maid had used that morning. He also wondered how often she came to the country estate.

From the manner in which she had arrived, Robert knew immediately she spent far more time at Ritchfield Park than he had over the years. She knew the servant's names, gave orders that sounded more like requests, and... what was that about seeing to it Perkins had more pay at the end of the month? Simply because the footman retrieved her trunk on an especially snowy day?

He wondered how much she expected the coach driver to receive for bringing her here all the way from London.

Robert considered his own experience only the day before.

To have paid witness to Graves' visible reaction to his arrival was almost worth the inconvenience of having traveled on what had to be the worst winter day in history. He was quite sure the butler hadn't so much as moved a facial muscle in his five decades, so seeing his widened eyes and opened mouth had been rather amusing. After all, it hadn't been *that* long since he'd spent time at his country estate.

Well, that wasn't exactly true. A year at least. Maybe three. More like...

Robert shook his head. Could it have been five years since his last visit to Ritchfield Park? It was no wonder he was feeling out of sorts of late. Bored with life in York. Bothered by the ghosts of his past.

Lonely.

He drew a hand down over his face, wincing when he felt the telltale signs he hadn't shaved that morning. He would have had his valet do it, but he had left the servant behind in York.

He wasn't sure now why he thought spending the Christmas holiday at Ritchfield Park would be a good idea. Rattling about in Gladstone Hall, the large manor house his family had owned for over three centuries a mile south of the walls of York, had felt as if he was communing with ghosts.

Then there had been the moment he noticed the housekeeper. Seeing her bruised face had truly brought out the ghosts of the past as well as a rage he didn't know he possessed. All that anger channeled into his fists until the butler was left battered on the floor of his office.

If he hadn't been a peer of the realm, he would have been arrested for the assault—that is, if Hartfield had even told anyone why he was dismissed from Gladstone Hall.

In an effort to recover his wits, Robert had retreated to his study. A different sort of ghost haunted him when he found a stash of long forgotten letters.

Letters from her.

A change of scenery—a change of venue—was necessary.

*G*lancing out the frosted study window to see only white was definitely a change. Robert didn't think he had ever seen so much snow in his entire life. Given the bone chilling temperatures beyond the wavy glass pane, he knew the stuff wasn't about to melt anytime soon.

At least the study was warm. Graves had seen to a roaring fire, the split logs a welcome change from the coal he had come to despise in York. Out here, wood fueled the fires that kept houses warm.

Coal might have made his earldom rich, but that didn't mean he had to like it.

Settling into the worn leather chair at his mahogany desk, Richard helped himself to a finger's worth of brandy from the crystal decanter behind his desk. His thoughts once again went to his wife as he took the first sip.

Why had she come to Ritchfield Park? She had to have left London on one of the worst days of winter and spent at least three nights at coaching inns along the way. He had a thought most were closed this time of year, although the mail coaches probably kept a few in business.

Then there was always the risk of running into a highwayman, of being robbed at gunpoint. They probably weren't so much of a problem in the winter, he thought, the reduced traffic on the roads along with the snow, cold, and wind all factors to discourage a would-be thief.

So why had Ivy made the trek in the first place? Why put her driver at risk of frostbite or worse? Risk the horses and her traveling coach?

She obviously hadn't guessed he would be in residence. Not that she would mind, he supposed. They always managed a rather civil union when they were both in residence in London. They were cordial over dinner and at entertainments when invitations forced them to attend together. They never raised their voices with one another. Never argued or fought.

They just... were.

He glanced over at the stack of papers and ledgers he had brought with him from Gladstone Hall. Most were invoices—expenses for the two coal mines, household bills from both Gladstone and Ritchfield Park, and one from his tailor. Thumbing through them, he paused and wondered at the lack of invoices from a modiste or frippery shop in London.

Opening a ledger covered in worn leather, he paged through the past year's entries in search of anything Ivy might have purchased and discovered that other than her monthly allowance, there wasn't a single expense he could attribute to her.

Was she actually using her pin money to pay the modiste?

To pay for hats and gloves and shoes? From where had she procured the beautiful redingote she had been wearing upon her arrival? The hat, both ridiculous as well as stunning given how well it matched her traveling clothes?

Robert was about to call for Graves to request she come to the study before he caught himself.

She hadn't sent word ahead she would be at Ritchfield Park—at least, if she had, Graves hadn't said anything about it. Surely the butler would have mentioned her imminent arrival had he known.

Did she usually come to the country estate for Christmas?

He shook his head, deciding he would discover the answer over dinner that evening.

After seeing to writing a number of cheques for the invoices, updating the ledgers for each property and the coal mines, and preparing the payments for the post, he leaned back and finished off his brandy.

His thoughts once again turned to Ivy. Curiosity finally getting the better of him, Robert moved to the door and called for Graves.

The butler appeared a moment later. "My lord?"

Robert motioned for him to come into the study and then shut the door, noting how the butler's eyes widened with alarm.

Did the servant think he was about to be sacked?

Robert kept his voice low when he asked, "Did you know her ladyship would be in residence this week?"

Graves shook his head. "I did not, my lord. She has come here for Christmas in the past, though. Many times. But if she sent word ahead she would be here this year, it did not arrive before the snow. We've not received the post in two days."

Furrowing a graying brow, Robert considered this bit of information for a moment before he asked, "Will it be a problem? For the cook, I mean?" He allowed his concern to show. "I apologize for not having given it a thought before, but is there enough in the pantry to feed us and all the servants for... say a fortnight? Enough wood for the extra fires?"

Apparently relieved by the line of questioning, Graves relaxed and said, "Oh, yes, my lord. Her ladyship brought provisions from London. Several crates from Fortnum and Mason along with gifts for the household staff."

"She did?" Robert couldn't help the tone of incredulity that sounded in his voice.

"Oh, yes, my lord. She was concerned the winter weather might have prevented cook from securing what she needed for this week's dinners and for the Twelfth Night festivities."

For a moment, Robert felt a stab of guilt over not having given his last-minute visit a thought as to how it would affect the staff at Ritchfield Park. "And the gifts?" He hadn't thought about those, either.

"The footman brought a ham, a side of beef, and a variety of vegetables we don't usually find here," Graves explained. "There are a number of other gifts, too, but they're to be placed in pasteboard boxes, my lord."

Robert glanced back at the desk. He couldn't recall any invoices from the high-end London grocer nor from any butchers. "And yet I rather doubt I'll be receiving an invoice for any of it," he murmured absently.

"My lord?"

"Nothing," Robert said, giving his head a shake. "Actually, what might be put inside those pasteboard boxes?" he asked in a quiet voice.

The butler seemed reluctant to answer at first, but then he leaned forward and whispered, "Oranges, my lord. Three in each box." He straightened. "There's another crate of oranges, as well, my lord. Always a favorite here at Ritchfield Park."

Robert furrowed a brow, but tried not to appear annoyed. "Where might I find her ladyship now?"

Graves appeared uncertain of how to respond. "She has been upstairs in the mistress suite since her arrival." He paused, his gaze darting to the side. "She had some concerns regarding your presence, my lord. Asked if you were entertaining a guest or if you might be expecting one or more to arrive for the Christmastide," he explained. "I told her I was not made aware you had invited anyone."

It was apparent the butler was curious, and Robert knew Graves would never ask him outright about his plans to entertain. House parties at Christmastide were rather unusual, though, and of course he would have warned the staff had he intended to host some friends.

He suddenly reconsidered the butler's words and felt heat color his cheeks. Had Ivy actually thought he would bring a doxy to Ritchfield Park? Or expect one to show up? "Is *she* expecting someone?" he asked, suspicion evident in his voice.

"She is not, my lord. Said the younger boy is still away on his Grand Tour, the older one has only recently returned, and that your daughters would be spending the holidays with their families in Devonshire and in Rome this year."

A stab of guilt had Robert nearly rolling his eyes. Both his sons, Michael and Charles, had graduated from Oxford in the last couple of years, and given the war against France, Michael had left on a ship bound for Greece rather than take the land route over the Continent. A year later, Charles, in an effort to avoid the wars, had joined his brother in Athens for a time before Michael returned to England. Charles was now concentrating his travels in countries along the coast of the eastern Mediterranean.

Meanwhile, the two daughters, both older than their brothers, had married heirs of the aristocracy. Charity's husband was a duke's son while Grace was married to an earl. Both had already become mothers.

Although he had met one of the grand babies—a future duke—he hadn't yet been introduced to the future earl. Grace and her husband were still on their wedding trip. The last he had heard, the couple had adopted Rome as a temporary home and were waiting to return to England until after their second baby was born.

If they weren't careful, she would be expecting her third on the way back to England.

Rome seemed to have that effect on young couples.

"Her ladyship is prepared to return to London should you wish to have the house to yourself, my lord," Graves said, interrupting Robert's brief reverie.

Robert scoffed. "I'll not have her traveling in this awful weather," he responded.

"I'll inform her—"

"I'll do it," Robert stated. "I have matters to discuss with her. 'Bout time I spoke with her in person."

Graves seemed momentarily confused. "Yes, my lord. Will there be anything else?"

Robert was sure he was missing something. At his townhouse in York, the housekeeper saw to all the particulars of running the household. "We'll need a menu for dinner," he remembered.

"Her ladyship has already provided cook with menus for the next fortnight, my lord," Graves replied.

Robert resisted the urge to roll his eyes again. "Of course she has," he murmured. He turned and indicated the pile of envelopes on the silver salver on his desk. "Should a mail coach manage to make it here through all the snow, those are ready for the post."

"I'll see to them, my lord." Graves helped himself to the salver and hurried toward the door.

Remembering it was nearly Christmas, Robert held up a finger. "What about greenery and... and a Yule log for the fireplace?"

Graves stopped in his tracks. "Already cut and ready to be brought in on the morrow, my lord."

Impressed, Robert crossed his arms and regarded the butler with appreciation. "In all this snow?"

Graves lifted a shoulder. "I had the footman see to it before the snow worsened, my lord."

"Good man," the earl stated. "I suppose I didn't come here for Christmas for it not to look like Christmas," he murmured.

"Of course not, my lord." Graves bowed his head and took his leave of the study.

Robert watched the servant depart and realized he no longer had any excuses to avoid Ivy.

Girding his loins, he headed for the stairs.

CHAPTER 3
A DRIVER RETURNS

Meanwhile, in the stable

Despite the snow and cold, Tom Walker had the traveling coach pulled up next to the stable and carriage house only moments after Perkins had unloaded Lady Ritchfield's trunk. The footman came out of the back door of the house to retrieve another trunk, this one from the interior of the coach.

The trunk containing what Tom knew to be oranges.

"Careful with that one," he warned. "Your Christmas present is in there."

Perkins' face lit up. "Oranges," he said with excitement. He hefted the trunk by the handles and disappeared into the house.

The other trunks atop the traveling coach held the rest of what the countess had brought for the household—mostly foodstuffs including a side of beef and a huge ham.

Bobby Ashton, the groom who saw to the two horses kept in residence at Ritchfield Park for the servants' use, hurried out to join Tom in unhitching the four Cleveland Bays. "How are you not frozen to death?" he called out, his own fingers numb from the cold. He had been hauling hay down from the rafters and feeding the horses when the coach appeared as if from a cloud as visibility worsened.

"Who says I am not?" Tom replied. He cursed softly under his breath as he undid the leather leads and led the first horse into the stable. Given his age—he was nearly fifty—it had been irresponsible of him to have pressed on in the bad weather. He couldn't imagine spending another night in a coaching inn, though. Not when they were so close to Ritchfield Park.

So close to Anne.

Perkins exited the house again, and Bobby helped him remove one of the trunks from atop the coach before he resumed helping with the horses.

The smell of pine assaulted Tom's nostrils as he entered the stable, and a quick glance into the first stall had him realizing why—it was filled with pine boughs.

Apparently the servants had already seen to acquiring the necessary greenery for decorating the house on Christmas Eve. Along the front wall of the stable lay a huge log, its branches trimmed away.

"The Yule log," he said in surprise.

"Indeed. Perkins cut it last summer so it would be ready," Bobby replied as he led the second horse into the next available stall. "Oh, and Clara has coffee in the kitchens," he added, referring to the cook. "And there's an empty bedchamber for you up in the servants' quarters, so you won't have to share."

"Where are you going to sleep?" Tom teased, heading back out to get the next horse.

Bobby chuckled. "With Christina, of course."

Tom halted in his tracks, looking back in surprise. "The housemaid?"

Nodding, Bobby displayed a huge grin. "She married me. Last spring," he said proudly.

The driver resumed his work to unhitch another horse. "Congratulations," he said as he experienced a pang of jealousy.

"Graves let us have the larger quarters upstairs, which is why there's a room for you," the groom explained.

Tom hoped he wouldn't be spending the night in the servant's quarters Bobby mentioned. He would leave his small trunk in there, of course, but he hoped he might be welcome in a certain housemaid's bed. "Any new servants on staff since last year?" he asked.

Leading the last horse into a stall, Bobby shook his head. "Nah. But Perkins almost quit—he and Graves don't always see eye-to-eye—but they kissed and made up."

Smirking at the groom's comment, Tom thought to scold the boy. Had he worked in the city, his words would have been misconstrued, and the servants might have suffered censure or worse. Out in the country, they were merely a tease. "Any gossip I should know about?"

Bobby used a pitchfork to load hay into the horse stalls while Tom saw to refilling the grain buckets. "The scullery maid married the parson's son, but she still comes to help Clara."

"All that way?"

"It's not far. Her man, Mr. Godfrey, has a farm just down the road."

The two finished seeing to the horses and moved to the carriage house, Bobby pulling one of the doors open as Tom saw to the other. With only an old phaeton, a gig, and the dog cart used by the servants, there was plenty of room for the countess' traveling coach. They struggled to remove the last trunk from atop it before moving it into the remaining space, the physical labor warming Tom enough so his hands and fingers regained their feeling. He winced at experiencing the familiar pins-and-needles sensation, though.

Removing his small trunk from the top of the coach, he hefted it onto his shoulder. "Grab my valise, will you?" he said, pointing to the leather bag he had left on the driver's seat.

Bobby did his bidding as Perkins saw to the last trunk. "Did you bring much from London?" he asked, hope in his voice.

Tom guffawed as they made their way to the back door of the country house. "Plenty. I was with her ladyship when she went shopping. She is a most generous woman."

"Well, that's good to hear," Bobby said, opening the door. He allowed Tom to step through before following him in. "'Cuz his lordship didn't seem to bring anything with him but his clothes."

This last was said with a hint of disgust, and Tom caught the tone. "Careful, boy. You don't know what was in his trunks," he warned.

Although he had worked for the earl for nearly twenty years before remaining in London to drive the countess for the past decade, Tom had paid witness to the earl and countess' life, first as a young couple in love, then as parents of four children, and now as older people who no longer spent much time in each other's company.

Having been married to one of the cooks at the townhouse in London and then widowed years ago, Tom knew the joy and heartbreak of marriage. He had mourned the loss of Mariel for several years and never thought to remarry, but when Lady Ritchfield had last traveled to the country estate for Christmas, he had become acquainted with Anne Salisbury.

The day after the Twelfth Night celebration when he had finished loading her ladyship's trunks onto the back of the traveling coach and his own onto the top, Anne had joined him outside.

With only a shawl wrapped about her shoulders against the winter chill, she had asked if she might write to him.

The simple query had him flustered at first. No one outside of his immediate family ever wrote letters to him, and those were few and far between.

He agreed, of course, and before he quite knew what was happening, Anne had stood on tiptoes and kissed him on the corner of his mouth.

He remembered blinking. Remembered her look of uncertainty. Remembered smiling. And finally he remembered gathering her into his arms and kissing her on the lips.

Although it had been hard to part from her after that, he didn't remember anything but that kiss for the entire trip back to London, his thoughts only on her. In the intervening year, he continued to think of her nearly every day, and more often on the days when the post would bring him a letter from her. He did his best in responding, his ability to write hampered by his limited writing skills.

The notes were short, a single page, and sometimes tucked into the missives from Graves directed to Lady Ritchfield. Anne's letters, chaste until the last sentence, where she would mention how much she looked forward to his return to Ritchfield Park, detailed life at the country estate and her thoughts of what she might do next in life.

At no point in any of her letters had Anne mentioned Bobby marrying Christina. Which is why, before they stepped into the kitchen, Tom said, "Does Miss Salisbury know you're married?"

Bobby glanced up at him with a look of confusion. "I should hope so. She was one of the witnesses at our wedding."

Tom furrowed a brow. "Huh," he responded before turning

his attention to Clara. He gave her a tentative grin, afraid she might scold him for the puddles he feared were being formed around his boots. "Miss Clara, it's good to see you again. I hear you have coffee."

The rosy-cheeked woman grinned and held out a mug in his direction. "I do indeed, Mr. Walker. I've also got some cheese and bread for you, since you're probably starvin' from the cold," she said, hurrying from the stove. "Why, you look positively frozen."

Tom thanked her and set his trunk on the nearby table before taking the proffered drink. Holding the cup between his hands to warm them, he motioned to where Perkins had left the two trunks he had brought in. "Her ladyship went shopping for you," he said.

"Aye, and I'll be unpacking them both shortly, young man, but first you're going to tell me all the gossip from London." She patted a chair at the table and took the one adjacent to it.

Snorting at hearing Clara refer to Tom as a young man, Bobby gave him a grin and said, "I'll take your trunk upstairs, old man."

Directing a beseeching look at the groom, Tom realized it would be some time before he could reunite with Anne.

CHAPTER 4
A COUPLE'S CONVERSATION

Meanwhile, in the mistress suite of Ritchfield Park

For the first time since leaving London, Ivy wished she had brought her lady's maid along. Although she didn't mind unpacking trunks and putting away clothes, she didn't want to have to repack them should she learn Robert intended to entertain a guest or two.

Chiding herself for not having thought to send a note letting him know she planned to be at Ritchfield Park for Christmas, Ivy pulled out the gown she planned to wear for dinner along with the matching jewelry and slippers.

The satin wasn't the least bit forgiving when it came to her hourglass-shaped body. Her strongest stays and at least one petticoat would be required.

Glancing out the window, she gave a start at seeing how much snow had fallen since her arrival. For as far as she could see, everything was white.

If Robert did intend to host a guest, they would have had to be on their way or almost to Ritchfield Park or they would become stranded. She rather doubted the roads were still passable, and snow was still falling.

She had never known Robert to want to host a house party. He didn't like attending them—he didn't care to play parlor games or pall mall—so he had never asked her to arrange one on his behalf.

But that didn't mean he was averse to having a guest spend a week or so. She had already imagined who that guest might be. Not his usual professor from Oxford or an old classmate from his university days, but rather a mistress. Or a perhaps a lady of the evening, one who lived nearby and who didn't work in a brothel but rather made house calls.

Ivy couldn't imagine a woman making the trek to Ritchfield Park in this weather, but she wouldn't put anything past someone who needed blunt to make their way in the world.

Oh, why hadn't she given a thought to the possibility her husband might wish to spend the Christmastide at Ritchfield Park? Ever since she had decided to remain in London instead of returning to York after the end of a Season every year, Ivy had come to the country estate for Christmas. Robert Strathford hadn't been to Ritchfield Park for Christmas in a decade. The last time he had made the trip, he had been there to hunt with the boys, but that had been at least five years ago, and she had been in London at the time with the girls.

Depending on their school schedules, sometimes one or more of her children would join her for Christmas. With all of them out of the country or married off with families of their own, she assumed she would be spending this year alone.

She might still if Robert had a guest coming. The thought of telling Mr. Walker they would be heading back to London sooner than expected had her wincing, though. He had so looked forward to the stay at the country estate—in fact, it had been him who insisted they finish the trek today rather than spend the night at the last coaching inn. She had been anxious to get to the country estate, too, even if she didn't have a paramour with whom to spend the cold winter nights.

The thought of decorating Ritchfield Park for the holiday still held a good deal of appeal, even if Robert and his lover were ensconced in one of the rooms of the country house.

She tried to imagine him with another woman, curious as to his preference for age. Would she be younger than him? Much younger? What about her hair color? Red, no doubt. She was sure her hair is what had caught his attention the first time he saw her.

Or perhaps it was her bosom. Surely he would choose a mistress blessed with bountiful breasts the size of melons. She could imagine how he would be hypnotized when they bounced about as he tumbled her, the nipples giving him something to concentrate on until his orgasm had him ceasing his movements and groaning his pleasure into them as he covered one with his mouth.

Ivy shivered at the reminder of the last time they had made love. The last time he had entered the mistress suite in the Mayfair townhouse. He hadn't said a word, but then, she wouldn't have expected words. He had simply needed her, and despite the fact that they hadn't spoken to one another for an entire day or more, she had welcomed him into her bed.

He hadn't kissed her that night. At least, not on the lips. He had kissed her nipples, though, and nibbled her neck. Pressed his lips to her belly, and he had maybe left a peck or two on her thighs.

Frissons shot through her body as she recalled that night, the last night before he once again left for York after another Season was complete.

She had woken to discover he was already gone.

Wiping away a tear, Ivy once again moved to the window. Gazing out, she hoped the snow wouldn't prevent the footman from being able to bring pine boughs and a

Yule log into the house on Christmas Eve. Perkins would then cut lengths of wire so the housemaids and cook could help with making a few wreaths and with stringing pine boughs atop mantels and on the staircase bannisters. By the time the red ribbon bows were added, the country house would look festive for the holiday and smell like a forest.

A knock at her door had her thinking Graves had returned with an answer to her question. "Come," she called out, turning from the window to discover her husband staring at her. "Hello," she managed, although she seemed to have lost her breath for a moment. "I can leave—"

"You are not going anywhere," Robert stated, his edict spoken in his most commanding voice. "Not that you could given this awful weather," he added, holding up a hand as if staving off an attack.

"But... what about your guest? Or... or guests?" she stammered.

He gave a start, obviously not expecting such a query. "There are no guests scheduled," he said, moving deeper into the bedchamber. He suddenly stopped, his eyes rounding. "Were *you* expecting... anyone?" he ventured. "Were you planning to host a... a house party perhaps?"

Ivy shook her head. "Goodness, no, Ritchfield. Our children are all grown and gone from the nest, so it's just me these days."

He nodded and looked as if he was having trouble deciding what to say next. "I... I met our oldest grandson," he suddenly blurted.

Her eyes widened. "The future duke?" she asked, grinning. "I can't say I was very thrilled with his name," she commented.

His brows furrowed. "Abraham?" he asked, as if he was struggling to remember the boy's moniker. "It's his other grandfather's name. And besides, everyone will simply call him by his current title until he inherits," he reasoned.

"That's the name I was referring to," she said with a smirk.

For a moment, Robert didn't seem to follow, and then he grimaced. "Viscount Ham. Oh, I see what you mean. He is a bit of a porker, though."

"Ritchfield," she scolded, although if pressed, she would have to agree the young boy was taking after his other grandfather. The man was rather rotund. At least Charity's husband, Luke, was still on the leaner side.

"He was just so... pudgy," Robert claimed.

Ivy did her best to suppress a chuckle.

They stared at one another for a moment before Ivy said, "I can't help but think my arrival interrupted something... important."

He shook his head. "Hardly. I brought all my paperwork with me, so I was just paying bills," he explained with a shrug of one shoulder.

The chill from the window had her moving closer to him. "Is... everything all right?" she asked, as if she feared poking a sleeping bear.

"Oh, it's fine," he assured her. "We're still... wealthy, if that's what you're asking."

Ivy had to suppress the urge to scoff. "I wasn't."

He dipped his head before adding, "But that does bring up a matter I wished to discuss with you."

She stiffened. "Oh?" For a moment, her heart felt as if it had dropped into her stomach. He was there to let her know he had decided to do something more permanent about their estrangement. Some sort of formal separation, no doubt.

Divorce, perhaps?

She couldn't imagine what her life would become should he do so. He would be generous, though—she wouldn't be left without an income—but the scandal would require she leave

London. Move to a cottage by the sea or the dowager house near York.

They had never talked about divorce. Never broached the subject even in casual conversation. But should he wish it, his title would most certainly ensure he would be granted a divorce.

Once again, Ivy was nearly in tears as she considered what her future might hold. "And what matter might that be?" she asked, her voice quavering.

"It's about your lack of spending."

Blinking several times, which had a tear escaping to run down her cheek, Ivy was tempted to ask him to repeat himself. She was sure she heard him clearly, though. "My... my lack of spending?" she repeated, her eyes widening in disbelief.

Well, this was unexpected. What man in the entire world would bring up his wife's thriftiness as a matter of discussion? He gave her a generous allowance, one which she didn't always spend because there were some months—especially those outside of the Season—she couldn't begin to. She had spent this month's allowance, though, the funds going toward the provisions and gifts she had brought with her for her stay at Ritchfield Park.

Robert held up a staying hand. "I am not *complaining*. Not in the least," he assured her. "But, my darling, you are a countess. *My* countess," he stated.

Recoiling at the vehemence in his claim, Ivy blinked. She couldn't recall him ever sounding so possessive.

"And I shouldn't want you to be... *economizing* if you thought I would be angered by an occasional bill from a modiste... or a hat shop, or... or Fortnum and Mason," he explained. "Because... because I wouldn't be," he stammered.

Ivy stared at him, her mouth slightly open, especially after the rather specific mention of the grocer from which she had purchased the oranges. "You give me an allowance every month, which more than covers the occasional bill from a modiste or the cost of a hat," she countered.

"And apparently provisions for this house as well as gifts for the servants," he said, arching a brow as if in disapproval.

It was Ivy's turn to lift a staying hand. "Oh, you will be receiving the invoice for the oranges," she stated in a scolding voice.

Robert couldn't help but grin at seeing her indignant expression. "Good," he stated. "And thank you for thinking of the pantry. For doing the menus," he added.

She gave him a tentative grin. "You're welcome, although it is my job to do," she reasoned. "That and seeing to the hanging of the greens, which I hope shall happen on the morrow."

Visibly relaxing at hearing her plans, Robert said, "It will. Graves assures me the servants have already collected the greenery. It's in the stable along with a suitable Yule log," he explained, watching for her reaction.

Ivy beamed in delight. "Oh, thank you for thinking to ask, Ritchfield." She paused, as if she feared his answer to her next question.

"What is it?" he prompted. He took a step closer.

"Are you... staying? For Christmas? For the Twelfth Night ceremony?"

He allowed a shrug. "I doubt I could leave any sooner, given the snow."

She allowed a wan smile. "So... that means you will be at dinner this evening?" she asked, hoping her query sounded like an invitation.

He nodded. "I will. And you?"

For a moment, she felt panicked. "I will be there, of course. I asked that dinner be served at six o'clock." Her gaze darted to the window. The gray snow clouds hid any evidence of the sun, and darkness was already descending over the countryside. "I like it earlier out here in the country, especially when it grows dark so soon this time of the year. Do you mind?"

He shook his head. "Six o'clock is fine." He paused, his manner uncertain. "In fact, I'll... I'll escort you down," he offered.

Ivy nodded. "Very well. Until then... I'll be in here, seeing to my clothes."

He frowned as he glanced around the bedchamber. "You didn't bring your lady's maid with you?"

Having pensioned the woman a day before leaving London, Ivy hesitated to respond. She had intended to write him a note explaining the situation during her time at Ritchfield Park, and although right now might have been the time to discuss it with him, she thought better of it. "I didn't bring Watkins. She has family in London, so I left her behind."

He continued to frown. "What will you do without her?" he asked, sounding alarmed.

She chuckled. "Oh, Ritchfield, I can dress myself," she said before pausing. "Mostly. But one of the housemaids here does a decent job with my hair, so it all works out." She paused a moment. "Did you bring your valet?"

He shook his head. "I did not. I, uh, I might regret it, but—"

"Well, if you need help shaving..." She allowed a shrug. "I recall a time I did a decent job of it," she murmured. "At least, I don't remember there being any bloodshed."

Chuckling softly, Robert rubbed a hand over the side of his face, deciding he would do it himself before dinner. "Perhaps in the morning," he replied, moving to the door. "Have a good afternoon, Ivy."

"You as well," she replied.

Ivy watched him depart and let out an audible sigh of relief when she no longer heard his footsteps in the corridor.

This next fortnight would be a long one, it seemed, but at least she would have a project to do on the morrow with seeing to the decorating for Christmas.

As for the rest of the time, well, she had planned to spend some of it writing correspondence and the rest reading in the library. Other than at meals, she probably wouldn't see her husband.

Which was probably just as well.

eanwhile, down on the first floor in the Ritchfield Park library

Hurrying to complete her duties on the first floor, Anne Salisbury swept the ash from the library's fireplace into a dustpan and dumped the contents into a can. She set several logs into place on the iron grate, knowing Graves would be up soon to light them.

The master was in residence for the first time in a long time, and Graves insisted the room be thoroughly dusted and ready for his visit. So far, the earl had kept to his study, but it was only a matter of time before Lord Ritchfield sought refuge in what was usually the warmest room of the house.

About to remind the butler she cleaned the library every day but Sunday, Anne had instead dipped a curtsy and went about her day in the usual manner. The parlor was always first followed by the gaming room, two enfilades, a drawing room, and then finally the library.

She had been in the middle of dusting one of the guest apartments when she heard the commotion of another arrival downstairs. For a moment, she thought she even felt the blast of cold air when the door was opened, but she had been standing near the fireplace and decided it was probably a gust of wind from the flue.

Moving to the window, she pulled back the drapes and angled her head in an effort to see if there was a coach in the drive. The vantage was wrong, though, for she couldn't make out anything more than the tracks in the snow. Hurrying to the door, she was about to head down the corridor to another room when she spotted Perkins, the footman, hefting a trunk up the stairs. He didn't pause in his climb, continuing to the second floor.

Not a guest, then, for a guest of the earl would have been assigned to stay in one of the *enfilades* on this floor. Which meant...

"Lady Ritchfield," she breathed.

She had spent the day before in anticipation of the countess' arrival. Or rather, the arrival of the man who would be driving Ivy Strathford, Countess of Ritchfield, to Ritchfield Park. For the entire time Anne had been a housemaid at the country estate, the countess came every Christmastide and always stayed until after the Twelfth Night festivities concluded. Every time, it was Tom Walker who drove her ladyship's traveling coach, and he had been doing so ever since the earl had married Ivy Merriweather in 1785.

Thirty years, Anne thought on a sigh. *He started driving her when I was but five years old.* She tried to remember what she had been doing when she was five. Certainly not thinking she might someday feel affection for a man who was fifteen years her senior.

She quickly finished her duties in the apartment and moved on to the drawing room. Tom would have to unhitch the horses and put away the traveling coach before she could expect him to come up the back stairs.

Given the time of day, he would probably stop at the

kitchens for a bite to eat, which meant Clara would demand news from London and it would be another half-hour or more before he could make his way upstairs.

She returned to the library and had just finished setting the logs when she heard someone on the servants' stairs at the end of the hall.

Grabbing the can of ashes and her feather duster, she rushed from the library, nearly colliding with the groom, Bobby, as he carried a small trunk up the narrow stairway.

"Careful there," he warned.

"Apologies," she whispered. "Whose trunk do you carry?"

He paused on the stairs. "Belongs to Mr. Walker. He and her ladyship are back in residence," he replied before resuming his climb.

Anne beamed in delight and then frowned when she realized she still needed to go downstairs to throw out the ashes. Despite Graves' annoyance at the mess they made by the back door, the servants had been spreading them on the walkways from the kitchen to the stable to help with traction on the ice. They had been using sand earlier in the winter, but with the supply running low, Graves insisted it be kept for use on the kitchen floor and by the hearth.

"Is he all right?" she asked.

Bobby once again paused on the stairs and glanced down at her. "A bit frozen, but he's thawing in the kitchen now," he said. "Clara's got his attention. Wants her report of gossip from London 'afore she'll let him out."

For a moment, Anne felt a pang of jealousy. The cook would probably spend more time in Tom Walker's company than she would be allowed on this day.

"By the way, you have something on your face," Bobby said, motioning with his free hand.

Anne inhaled sharply. "Soot, no doubt," she said, lifting a

hand to find her fingers black with it. When she glanced back up the stairs, Bobby had disappeared.

Although she wanted nothing more than to see Tom, she instead thought to wash her hands and face first. She left the ash can in the corner and made her way to her tiny room on the third floor.

Not bothering to shut her door once she was in her quarters—no other servants were about this time of the day—she lifted the looking glass her mother had given her from the washstand and regarded her reflection with a wince. The mirror wasn't very large, but it was enough to show her face was indeed smudged with soot. She moved to the washstand and cleaned her hands before wiping her face with a cloth.

While she held the mirror in one hand, she used the fingers of the other to smooth over her skin, wincing at seeing how much she had aged since joining the staff at Ritchfield Park. Wrinkles extended from the sides of her eyes, and the lines around her mouth seemed to have deepened. Although the skin over her cheeks was still smooth, there were faint worry lines between her eyebrows.

Would he notice?

About to set the looking glass back on the washstand, Anne froze in place when she realized she wasn't alone.

"Lady Ritchfield is asking for you," Graves said from just outside her door. "She has asked that you be her lady's maid whilst she's in residence."

A combination of excitement and disappointment had her hesitating as she stood to give the butler a curtsy. "Yes, Mr. Graves. I'll be right there," she said.

Finishing her ablutions, Anne made her way back down the servants' stairs and to the mistress suite.

Perhaps she would see Tom at supper.

CHAPTER 6
DRESSING FOR DINNER

A half hour later

Ivy watched Anne Salisbury gingerly insert another pin into the coiffure she had created, the woman's reflection in the dressing table mirror a study of concentration and concern.

"You're doing fine. You'll be a lady's maid in no time at all," Ivy said by way of encouragement. "In fact, I may have to take you back to London with me."

The housemaid's eyes widened in what appeared to be surprise. "Oh, I would like that very much, my lady," she replied.

The comment had Ivy smirking. "I know it's none of my business, but I am aware that you and Mr. Walker have formed an... attachment," she stammered. She heard Salisbury's sharp inhalation of breath and regarded the maid's reflection in the dressing table mirror, noting her momentary fright. "And I don't object in the least."

The maid's look of fear changed to wonder. "You don't?"

"Of course not. In fact, I believe I have you to thank for my being here today," she explained. "We really shouldn't have been traveling with the snow falling as it was," she added.

"Oh," Anne sighed. "It was a relief to learn you two had arrived, my lady."

Ivy's eyes widened. "Have you spoken with him?"

Anne's face displayed a blush. "I have not, my lady," she said, shaking her head. "Perhaps we'll have time later this evening to... to talk."

Grinning, Ivy turned on the tufted seat to regard the maid directly. "Oh, I do hope you two have time to do more than that," she teased. "That all goes well for the two of you," she added. "In fact..." She paused, her own face coloring with heat. "May I ask which rooms you see to in the house?"

About to insert another hairpin into the coiffure she was creating atop Ivy's head, Anne hesitated. "The first floor, my lady. The parlor, the drawing room, two apartments, and the library. And the corridor, of course."

Ivy turned back to face the dressing table mirror. "Well, since there are no guests in residence, I certainly wouldn't object if one of those apartments were... *occupied* for a time," she murmured. "Surreptitiously, of course. I shouldn't want any of the other servants to... to *discover* you and think they might be entitled to their use."

Anne's eyes rounded in surprise. "My lady?"

Once again turning on her seat, Ivy angled her head to one side. "It's nearly Christmas, and I think this house could use a bit of... romance," she whispered. "Goodness knows, it's been a a long time since there was any of that here at Ritchfield Park. If Walker and you are thinking of marriage, then I only wish to do my part to help."

Dipping her head, Anne allowed a tentative grin. "I thank you for your consideration, my lady. I cannot speak for Mr. Walker, but I am sure he, too, will be very appreciative of your offer."

"Well, as I said, do keep it quiet." She glanced at the clock. "Oh, it's already a quarter of the hour," she murmured. "Have you much more to do?"

Anne held up another pin. "Only a few more curls and I'll be done, my lady. I apologize if I am slow, but it's because I worry I will stab your head," she added, capturing her lower lip with a tooth as she inserted the pin into Ivy's flame red hair.

"Oh, I'll survive," Ivy said dryly, wishing her lady's maid in London had showed such concern for the skin on her head. Watkins was an efficient servant, but patience was not one of her virtues. Ivy was sure she sported scars on her scalp from the ferocity with which Watkins had inserted hairpins over the years.

She wouldn't regret her decision to pension the lady's maid, which reminded her she really needed to discuss the particulars with her husband over dinner that evening. She'd had the perfect moment in which to do it only the hour before, when Ritchfield had asked if she had left her lady's maid behind.

Why had she hesitated? He probably didn't care one whit who she employed as her lady's maid, but Watkins had been with the family since before he took Ivy to wife. She had been his mother's lady's maid, and then, before his sister had married, she had been her lady's maid. It didn't seem right to pension the woman without his permission. Without his blessing.

Remembering Ritchfield's unshaven face, she wondered if he had decided to pension his valet as well. Was that why the older servant hadn't come with him from York?

If he still employed Ferguson, the one he brought with him to London for the Season, then he was old enough to retire. Probably had been for a decade.

"I'm wondering how his lordship is doing without his

valet," Ivy said, hoping the housemaid would share any information she might have been privy to during the servant's breakfast that morning.

Anne glanced up to see Ivy regarding her reflection in the dressing table mirror. "I believe Graves is seeing to his lordship, my lady. He was quite surprised when Lord Ritchfield arrived yesterday," she remarked. "Apparently it's been quite some time since his lordship has been in residence here."

"Oh?" Ivy remarked. "So… Ritchfield didn't send word ahead he would be coming for Christmas?"

"No, my lady. From something Graves said, the earl's visit was not planned at all. In fact, he fears something happened in York," she said, keeping her voice low.

Ivy stiffened. None of their children lived in the city, so she didn't think it had anything to do with them. His mother and father had both died long ago, succumbing to the influenza epidemic of 1782, so they couldn't be the reason.

Had something happened in one of the coal mines? She knew Robert trusted the foremen—both lead foremen had been under his employ for years. If there had been an accident in one of the mines, surely she would have heard about it in the news.

She struggled to come up with another reason why Robert would flee York when the weather was so bad.

"What *exactly* did he say?" Ivy asked, turning to regard the housemaid directly.

Anne blinked a few times. She seemed reluctant to speak until Ivy's eyes widened with her impatience. "The ghosts of the past have driven me from York," she recited as if from memory.

Ivy jerked back on the small tufted seat. "Ghosts?" she repeated, not expecting such an answer.

Anne lifted a shoulder. "That's what Graves said his

lordship said, my lady," she affirmed. "Is the house in York haunted, perhaps?"

About to reply in the negative, Ivy considered the query a moment. She hadn't been to Gladstone Hall in a very long time. Almost a decade. Perhaps some ghosts had settled in during her absence. "I never encountered any whilst I lived at Gladstone Hall," she murmured. "But then, that's been years ago." *And only when I wasn't in London for the Season*, she didn't add.

The sudden knock at the door had them both reacting in shock until Ivy nervously tittered. The talk of ghosts obviously had them on edge. "Come," she called out. She turned her gaze back towards the mirror and watched her husband appear, framed in the opening door, as a reflection in the dressing table mirror.

She had to stifle the urge to inhale sharply before she allowed a look of awe. He had dressed for dinner, his formal clothes all black but for the white satin waistcoat embroidered with red leaves and berries. Even his shirt, cravat, and stockings were black, so the contrast with the waistcoat was stark.

For a moment, his expression seemed as severe as his clothing. Far too serious for one about to head down to dinner in a country house. Apparently the sight of her awe, reflected in the looking glass, caused him to soften his expression.

"You look surprised," he commented. "And rather lovely this evening."

Ivy couldn't believe how her body reacted. A frisson skittered down her spine and through her belly, which had her inhaling softly when the pleasure was at its peak. "Why, thank you," she said, coming to her feet. She slid them into the black slippers Anne had set out for her.

The housemaid immediately stepped back and dipped a curtsy before disappearing into the dressing room.

While Robert seemed surprised by Anne Salisbury's sudden departure, Ivy was not.

She knew there was a reunion in the maid's future, and she already knew how much the man involved was looking forward to it.

CHAPTER 7
A REUNION IS SWEET BUT SHORT

M eanwhile, in the kitchen
Having consumed two cups of coffee and all the bread and cheese Clara had offered him whilst sharing what gossip he knew from London, Tom Walker stood and begged forgiveness.

"It's been a long day, Clara, and I really need to be getting out of these damp clothes," he said by way of an excuse.

"Well, I need to be finishing the master's dinner," Clara replied. She had spent the time whilst Tom was regaling her with stories putting together the soup and main course for that night's dinner as well as the servants' supper. She had bustled about the kitchen for nearly an hour, wielding a wicked looking knife on a hunk of beef followed by some vegetables that didn't deserve the ferocity she showed them.

Now that everything seemed to be either on the stove or in the oven, she turned her attention to some apples. "Well, off with you then," she said, waving a gnarled hand in his direction.

Tom gathered his greatcoat, hat, and valise and headed up

the servants' stairs. He had just made it to the second-floor landing when a soft body collided with his.

"Ooof."

"Oh!"

He leaned back as far as he could in the tight, confined space of the stairwell at the same moment the woman who had joined him on the stairs took a step up to give him more room.

His eyes widened. "Anne?"

"Tom?"

The two stared at one another, their gazes level given she was up one step from the landing. "Aye," he said, finally blinking.

She inhaled sharply, and for a moment, neither of them moved.

All at once, her arms were around his neck, and Tom was forced to drop the valise so that he might steady himself by wrapping an arm around her. The bag tumbled down the steep stairs, bumping and thumping as Anne's lips found his.

Tom was sure he had never been kissed quite like Anne was kissing him, as if her life—and his—depended on it. Besides her soft, suckling lips, there were her fingers, which were doing their best to comb through every bit of hair he had left on his head.

If he had been feeling chilled from his damp shirt and waistcoat, he certainly wasn't now, what with her practically plastered to the front of his body. Her livery was probably growing just as damp, especially where her bosom pressed to his chest.

As for the rest of him, it still seemed it was in the process of catching up to what his mouth was doing, his hands dropping his greatcoat and hat to move to her waist. His nether region certainly understood what was happening, for his cock was rising to the occasion in a way it hadn't done in a very long time.

He hoped she wouldn't notice, but when her hips tilted against the bulge in his breeches, he broke off the kiss and struggled to catch his breath.

"I'm so glad to see you," he whispered.

"Obviously," she replied, a grin brightening her face, even in the darkened stairwell.

"Apologies, doll, but I cannot help—"

"Don't you dare apologize," she murmured. "Have you anywhere you must be?"

He glanced down the stairs. "I was going to wash up before, well, before I was going to come find you," he stammered.

"There's a guest bedchamber we can use on the first floor," she whispered.

"Anne..." he started to scold her.

"It's all right. Her ladyship gave us permission. I didn't even ask—not that I would—she just offered it. I think because she appreciates how quickly you got her here," she explained. "And..."

Tom chuckled softly. "She is a bit of a romantic," he murmured.

"No one else can know," she said in a quiet voice.

"Hello?" a voice called from below.

Anne was quick to step down and out of the stairwell, while Tom turned on the landing and said, "Who's there?"

Bobby appeared at the bottom of the stairs. "I take it this is yours?" he asked, holding up the valise.

"Aye," Tom said. "Trying to take up too much at once, I suppose," he said. He made a move to go back down the stairs, but Bobby was already on his way up.

"It's no bother. I wondered how long it would be 'afore Clara would let you out of the kitchen."

"Well, I'm free now," Tom sighed, bending to retrieve his hat and greatcoat. "You can show me which room I'm in, if you would," he added, giving Anne a pointed glance only a moment before Bobby joined him.

Anne ducked around the corner, and then, when she heard Lord Ritchfield's voice down the hall, she hurried into one of the guest bedchambers. She held her breath, hoping the commotion hadn't attracted the master's attention.

From the way he had been staring at Lady Ritchfield only a few moments earlier, she doubted he would have noticed. He was obviously besotted with his countess. His comment, *You look surprised and rather lovely this evening*, had come out sounding as if he might follow it up with a growl. Anne was sure he was about to tear her gown from her body and have his way with her right then and there.

She had escaped into the dressing room and scampered out of the connecting room as fast as she could.

Deciding she had waited long enough, she left the guest bedchamber and hurried up the stairs. Before she made it to the servants' floor, Bobby reappeared at the top of the stairs. He stepped aside to allow her off the stairs.

"Good afternoon," she said, giving him a nod.

"Afternoon," he acknowledged. "Have you seen Christina?"

She paused and furrowed a brow. "Not since this morning," she replied. "At breakfast."

He allowed a grunt of thanks and hurried down the stairs.

Waiting until she was sure he was gone, Anne made her way down the corridor until she came to one of the servant's rooms she knew was usually unoccupied. Knocking softly, she heard movement behind the wooden panel before it opened an inch.

"Yes?"

Anne blinked. "Christina?"

The young woman opened the door wider. "Yes, it's me," she said in a whisper.

"Bobby was just looking for you," Anne said, curious as to what the other housemaid was doing in the room Tom should have been in.

"I know," she said on a sigh. "I just wanted an afternoon to myself," Christina said, once again sighing as she moved to sit on the edge of the cot. It was obvious she had been napping.

"Well, if you're in here, then where do you suppose Mr. Walker is?"

"He's here?" Christina asked, her eyes widening in delight. "You must be so happy."

Anne nodded, but she glanced around nervously. "I am, but I would be happier if I knew where he was."

"Prob'ly in Bobby's old room."

Anne's gaze darted to the side. "I thought *this* was Bobby's old room," she whispered.

"This is *my* old room," Christina replied, grinning.

Confused, Anne asked, "Why didn't Bobby try to find you in here?"

"Who says he didn't?" Christina countered with a smirk. The two broke into a fit of giggles.

"I will leave you to your nap," Anne said finally, rising from the edge of the cot. "But you should know the earl and countess just went down for their dinner. Ours won't be long."

"Promise you won't tell Bobby?"

Anne turned and held up a pair of crossed fingers. "I promise," she replied. She pulled the door shut behind her.

She would have gone to Bobby's old room next, but Graves appeared at the top of the servants' stairs. "Cook has the staff supper ready," he said.

"Already?" Anne couldn't help the sound of incredulousness in her voice.

"His lord and ladyship are back in residence, so our schedules will be a bit different this next fortnight," Graves replied. "Might you know the whereabouts of Mrs. Ashton?"

Anne struggled to keep a straight face. "I do. I'll let her know about supper," she replied, sighing when she realized any other attempt to speak with Tom would have to wait until after supper.

CHAPTER 8
DINNER BREAKS DOWN BARRIERS

*E*arlier, in Ivy's bedchamber

Ivy gave a start as Anne Salisbury curtsied and quickly took her leave by way of the dressing room. Although the woman hadn't been formally dismissed, she had completed dressing her and her hair.

She had done a masterful job of it, too, the fiery copper locks pulled into a series of curls around her crown atop which lay a smooth, flat bun. Even better, her scalp hadn't suffered one whit.

The appearance of Robert had no doubt frightened poor Salisbury, and Ivy couldn't blame her. Her own heart was pounding a tattoo in her chest worthy of a Scottish drummer. Not due to fright so much—more because of the sudden excitement she felt at seeing him in his formal clothes.

"Skittish thing," Robert said, a frown marring his already harsh features.

"Oh, you meant Miss Salisbury?" Ivy teased, referring to his comment, *You look surprised and rather lovely this evening.*

He gave her a quelling glance.

"That skittish thing is the reason Walker got me here in

this awful weather," Ivy said, threading a sapphire earbob through the piercing in her ear.

Robert furrowed a brow. "What do you mean?"

Ivy dared a glance back at the dressing room to ensure Salisbury had indeed taken her leave. "Mr. Walker is sweet on her. They've been exchanging correspondence ever since they met last year," she explained, finishing with the other earbob.

"I thought Walker was a married man," Robert said, his voice nearly a whisper.

Turning from the mirror, Ivy frowned. "He was, until Mariel died five years ago," she said on a huff. She was about to add, "Do keep up," but from his stunned reaction, she thought it best not to scold him.

"I'm sorry. I... I didn't know," he murmured. "But I am happy for him... if..." He waved to the dressing room door. "If he and Salisbury..." He cleared his throat and sighed, obviously not about to say any more about it.

"Well, good, because I may have given them permission to..." She stopped speaking when she noticed how he was staring at her. "What is it?"

"You didn't have to go to all this trouble for me," he said, waving a hand, his gaze taking in her blue dinner gown, jewelry, and coiffure. "But I know you prefer to stick with tradition. You always look stunning in blue," he added.

Ivy grinned. "It's called sapphire, and it perfectly matches the parure you gave me for our tenth anniversary," she said, holding up a wrist to display a sapphire and diamond bracelet. The earbobs decorating her earlobes were part of the same set. "I so rarely have an occasion to wear the parure."

Robert gestured to the dressing room. "Will she be coming out of there?"

Ivy glanced to where he indicated. "I rather doubt it. There's a servant's entrance on the other side. Salisbury is long gone." She didn't add that she had a thought as to just where the servant was heading.

She hoped the woman was off to see Walker.

Given the timing of their arrival and the amount of time it would have taken for the driver to unhitch horses and when Graves would have summoned the housemaid to her bedchamber, Ivy knew the two wouldn't have yet had a chance to see one another.

He displayed a frown. "I didn't mean to scare her off," he murmured.

Realizing Ritchfield had given her the perfect opening with his comment, Ivy asked, "Did you bring some ghosts with you from York?" From the expression on his face, Ivy knew she had hit a nerve.

"Why... why do you ask that?" he stammered.

She stepped forward and hooked her hand around his elbow, forcing him to turn towards the door. "Why did you look as if you had seen one when I asked?" she countered in a quiet voice.

Robert stutter-stepped before he had them taking leave of her bedchamber. "Perhaps I was hoping to leave them behind," he murmured, once they were in the corridor.

Ivy gathered her skirts in one hand when they approached the top of the stairs. "What's happened, Robert? What ghosts are you talking about?" she asked in a whisper. Although there didn't appear to be any servants nearby, she didn't wish for their conversation to be overheard. From what Salisbury had said, she assumed all the servants had heard Graves' recite the comment about the ghosts. She didn't want them to think her husband had brought some of them with him to Ritchfield Park.

Robert was quiet until they reached the landing. "I found some correspondence I'd quite forgotten about," he said.

"Oh?" she prompted. They descended another flight of

stairs before she realized she would have to force an answer from him. "From whom?"

"You," he stated, the moment he reached the ground floor. He led them to the dining room as Ivy gasped and stared at him.

"Me?" she said in disbelief. "I… I haven't written letters to you in—"

"Years, yes, I'm well aware," he said, pulling out a chair for her at the end of the long dining table.

Ivy slowly settled into the chair, watching him as he made his way to the carver at the other end. She winced at seeing how far away from each other they would be sitting if she remained where she was. Coming to her feet, she waved to the footman. "Perkins, I'm going to sit there," she said, pointing to the chair adjacent to the carver.

The footman's eyes rounded. "Yes, my lady."

Ivy knew she had caught Robert off-guard with her edict, but she was determined to continue their conversation without worry the servants might eavesdrop. From Salisbury's comment a few minutes earlier, she knew the staff was curious about their master's unexpected appearance at the country estate.

The footman was quick to set up a place setting for her, and he held the chair until she was reseated. Meanwhile, Robert had remained standing behind the carver and finally sat down.

"You may serve the wine and the first course," Ivy said, directing the instructions to Perkins.

"Yes, my lady." The footman disappeared into the butler's pantry.

"I don't think we've ever sat this close to one another during dinner," Robert remarked, experimentally reaching out with his foot to determine where her slippered feet were under the table.

Ivy couldn't help the rush of heat that had her cheeks reddening and her insides tumbling about. "I don't wish to shout across the table when we're speaking of ghosts," she whispered, sounding far too defensive.

The footman appeared with the wine, and Graves delivered bowls of soup. When they were once again alone, Robert said, "The old letters aren't really the ghosts," he said, taking his spoon in hand. He stirred his soup a few times before lifting it to his lips. A purr of appreciation sounded.

Ivy furrowed an auburn brow when her gaze went to the hand that held his spoon. The knuckles there were scuffed, and one appeared larger than the others. "And yet they had you fleeing York," she accused, tearing her attention from his hand. "On the absolutely worst day of winter." She noticed his grimace and added, "What's happened, Robert? What's going on?"

He dipped his head, his gaze on the curls of steam rising from his bowl of soup. "I read them," he stated, before he took another spoonful of soup to his mouth. "Or reread them, I suppose." He ate the soup and didn't make eye contact as he returned the spoon to the bowl and once again stirred the contents.

"How old were these letters?" she asked, finally eating a spoonful of soup she had been holding in anticipation of his response.

"About thirty years, I suppose," he replied.

She reacted with surprise. "You have letters from me that are that old?"

He gave her a quelling glance. "Of course. I've kept all of them," he said. "You wrote the ones I was reading whilst I was in London for Parliament and you were in York. Moving into Gladstone Hall. Redecorating the salon and the dining room," he added wistfully.

Ivy inhaled softly. "Oh, I remember. We had just returned

from our wedding trip, and I was so happy." She suddenly frowned. "Except I wasn't."

He arched a dark brow in surprise. "You weren't?"

"Oh, I was happy, but I missed you terribly," she admitted. "We had spent every day together since our wedding and then... suddenly you were *gone*."

He considered her words as he took another spoonful of soup. "In one of the letters, you had learned you were with child," he said. "I think I must have bought drinks for everyone at Brooks's the night after I received that letter."

Grinning, Ivy continued eating her soup. "I feared you would be bored reading all my correspondence. I recall I wrote every day until I knew you had left London to come home."

"Indeed you did, but I was never bored, Ivy. Not whilst reading the letters anyway." He sighed. "I was never so glad to leave London as I was at the end of that session."

Ivy allowed a wan smile at hearing his claim. "I was so relieved when you arrived at Gladstone Hall. So I could show you what had been done to those rooms," she said wistfully. "I so wanted to see your reaction."

Robert winced, remembering he had only had eyes for her. "You must have thought me daft when I didn't immediately notice the changes."

She tittered. "*Blind*, is what I remember thinking," she countered, arching an auburn brow for emphasis.

"Only because I couldn't take my eyes off *you*," he argued. "You were already so round with child," he murmured, his gaze clearly on his mind's eye. "And you glowed, as if you had swallowed a lit candle."

Ivy grinned at the memory. "I was so worried you would find me too fleshy."

"God, no," he whispered. "You were so gorgeous. You still are," he said, waving his spoon for emphasis. "It's a good thing both Charity and Grace take after you more than me."

Staring at her husband for a moment, Ivy noted his thoughtful expression. "Thank you," she murmured.

He went on as if he hadn't heard her. "Our poor boys. I fear they've both taken after me in the looks department—"

"Our sons are quite striking in appearance," she argued. "There are a dozen young ladies who would be happy to wed them once they set their minds to marriage."

Robert winced. "I know I wasn't a handsome bloke—"

"You didn't need to be," she interrupted. When she noticed his questioning glance, she added, "You've always had a sort of charisma about you."

"Charisma?" he repeated in surprise. He dropped his spoon to stare at her.

She countered his stare with one of her own, her eyes finally narrowing. "An aura of... *power*, I suppose is what it is. As if you can command a room just by standing there," she explained. "It's probably due to your Scandinavian ancestry. Or maybe from a Roman centurion," she teased. "It was very effective. Still is, I think."

Robert settled back in his chair, his gaze darting about as if he was confused. He cleared his throat. "I certainly don't *feel* powerful," he murmured.

Having lifted a finger to direct the footman to clear the soup bowls, Ivy stared at him. "Why ever not?"

He waited until the footman had left the dining room to say, "I'm getting old, Ivy. I'm not the same man I was."

She inhaled softly. "I don't know what you're seeing in the mirror these days, but you don't appear to have aged one whit since the last time I saw you," she said.

"Have you considered wearing spectacles?" he asked, a smirk appearing to lighten his stark features.

Once again tittering, she waited until the footman and Graves had delivered the next courses—she had elected for several to be served together to shorten the meal time—before she said, "I cannot believe finding some old letters would have you fleeing Gladstone Hall to come to Ritchfield Park." She swallowed. "But I'm glad you did."

"You are?" he asked in surprise.

"Well, of course. I shouldn't want you to spend your Christmas alone in that huge house," she replied. "I recall it was rather drafty in the winter."

"Still is," he murmured. He selected a slice of beef and placed it on her plate before he helped himself to another for his plate.

Ivy watched as he filled her plate with a variety of food, her eyes rounding with each additional serving. "I am not with child, so I rather doubt I'm going to be able to eat all this," she warned.

He shrugged. "We have all night."

Her brows furrowing, Ivy tucked into her meal, secretly glad the meat wasn't the texture of shoe leather and the vegetables weren't mushy. "So... what exactly was it about the letters that bothered you so much?"

About to eat some beef, Robert put down his fork and shook his head. "Nothing *bothered* me," he claimed. "They were merely... reminders, I suppose."

Ivy paused her fork in midair, the peas on it threatening to roll off the tines. "Reminders?" she prompted.

"Of us. Of how happy we were," he explained, one shoulder lifting in a shrug. "Which had me wondering what happened to... to drive you away? To keep us apart except during the Season?" He sighed as if he was exasperated. "It feels as if it's been ten years since we were truly... together."

Ivy stopped chewing and nearly choked. She took a long draught of her wine. "Actually, it *has* been ten years, and as I recall, it's always been *you* who has left me," she said in a quiet voice.

Robert stiffened, as if he was preparing for an argument.

"I leave London, yes. We used to *all* go to York every year after Parliament was finished. The entire family. Then ten years ago I went back to York—I had to, what with the mines and all—and you weren't with me. You stayed in London," he accused.

Despite her desire to keep their conversation light, Ivy decided to argue her side of the matter. "As did the girls because that's when Charity started finishing school," she stated, referring to their oldest daughter. "I wasn't about to leave her alone in London," she explained. "We talked about it at the time."

Robert straightened in his chair. "Oh. I'd quite forgotten about that," he whispered. "But... you stayed again the next year," he accused.

"Because by then, both Charity and Grace were in finishing school," she replied. "And I stayed another three years until they were both done with school and their come-outs, and then there were their betrothals, and their weddings—"

"And yet you continued to live there, even after they were wed," he accused.

There it was. The words describing exactly when their estrangement had begun. The acknowledgement that something had gone wrong.

But how had this been her fault?

Ivy sighed and dipped her head. "As I recall, you no longer seemed to want my company," she said in a quiet voice. She managed to make the words less an accusation and more of an explanation.

"But... but I did," he assured her. He turned in his chair to face her, one hand covering hers.

Ivy's attention darted to his hand, her gaze going from his scuffed knuckles to the Ritchfield crest emblazoned on the onyx ring he wore on his fourth finger. For years, they had joked that should he punch someone on the chin, they would be left with a permanent scar the mirror image of the raised crest.

She lifted her other hand and traced the edges of the gold crest with a fingertip. "You never asked me to go to back to York with you. You just packed up and left the day after Parliament was over."

His mouth dropped open as he shook his head. "I didn't think you required an invitation to go back to your own home," he countered quietly.

Ivy inhaled to respond but instead simply stared at the ring.

Dipping his head, he said, "I suppose I should have asked you. Showed that I was *interested* in learning your plans," he admitted.

About to mention she hadn't joined him in York because she feared she might be interrupting an *affaire*—she had always worried he had taken a mistress—Ivy thought better of it and said, "I should have asked about yours."

Despite the seriousness of their discussion, Robert displayed an expression of amusement. "We are certainly a pair," he murmured.

Ivy sighed, her head dropping to one side. "Your life was in York. Mine was in London."

He pushed aside his dinner plate and leaned forward to place his elbows on the table. "What if... what if it wasn't?" he asked, steepling his fingers.

Ivy blinked. "Are you referring to my life? Or—"

"Either," he said. "Neither. Oh, I don't know. Does it really matter, if neither one of us wants to be in the other place?"

Ivy's eyes widened. "I didn't say I didn't wish to be in York," she said softly.

He once again dipped his head. "It's true I would rather be in York than in London," he admitted. "But... if you knew you were... *wanted* in York, would you come?"

Ivy stared at him for several seconds. "I... I suppose I would."

He swallowed. "Do you think you might be inclined to go there? After Christmas? Mayhap stay until..."

"Until it's time to go to London for the Season?" she asked in awe. Inhaling slowly, she blinked several times and resisted the urge to place a hand on his forehead to check for a fever. Her husband of nearly thirty years appeared paler than usual, which only exacerbated his harsh features and stern expression. "Robert? Are you feeling all right?"

He frowned, which worsened his appearance. "I'm fine. I'm merely..." He shook his head. "Lonely," he whispered.

"Robert," she said, the word almost a whisper.

He jerked at hearing his given name, as if he hadn't heard her use it several times already that evening. She almost always called him Ritchfield. "If you didn't go back to London —at least, not right away—would there be someone... anyone who would miss you there?" he asked.

Ivy recognized the opportunity to mention her desire to pension Watkins and to hire a replacement. "Only my lady's maid, and that's a topic I did wish to discuss with you."

Robert gave a start, obviously not expecting that particular answer. "I did wonder about that," he responded. "You seemed especially vexed about it when we spoke earlier. As if you wanted to say something but thought better of it."

"That's it exactly," she admitted.

He tossed his napkin onto the table. "Has something happened with Watkins?" he asked, his tone suggesting he was suspicious of the servant.

"I almost mentioned it upstairs," she admitted. "But I didn't wish to in case... well, because sometimes the walls have ears," she whispered. "And this is about a servant."

"Understood," he said. "Go on."

Ivy pushed aside her dinner plate. "She's grown old and

quite forceful with the hair pins," she stated. "I know she was your mother's maid, and your sister's, but..." She paused and winced.

"Go on," he urged.

"My scalp can no longer abide her attempts to stab it to death repeatedly twice a day, every day."

Blinking, Robert furrowed a brow. "Then by all means, pension the woman and hire a new one." He directed a thumb into the air. "That skittish one upstairs if you'd like. She can obviously style hair," he claimed, waving to her head. "Your coiffure looks especially fetching this evening."

Regarding him with an expression of surprise, Ivy finally sighed with relief. "Thank you. I shall do that," she said. Her brows suddenly furrowed. "Is that why you didn't bring your valet with you? Because he's nicking you with the razor?"

His gaze darting to one side, Robert sighed. "Well, Waddington isn't causing bloodshed," he replied. "At least, not every day, but he has grown long in the tooth, and he takes entirely too long to shave and dress me in the mornings."

Ivy tittered softly. "Well then pension him and hire a new one," she murmured.

Robert leaned back in his chair and crossed his arms, a grin lifting the corner of his mouth. "Thank you. I shall do that," he replied.

Ivy sighed contentedly and pulled her dinner plate back into place. She helped herself to another bite of beef. "I am happy to help."

"You always were," he remarked, placing his napkin back on his lap and returning his attention to his dinner.

It was another hour before the two took their leave of the dining room. Robert escorted her up the stairs and to the mistress suite. Although Ivy half expected he might ask to come to her bedchamber later that evening, he simply bade her goodnight with a kiss on her cheek. "I'm off to the library," he said. "See you in the morning for breakfast?"

Ivy managed to hide her surprise at hearing the query. "Breakfast, yes," she agreed. "I usually go down about nine o'clock."

"I'll see you then."

Once she had her door shut, she leaned against it and allowed a sigh of relief.

Or was it disappointment?

CHAPTER 9
SERVANTS RECEIVE THEIR ASSIGNMENTS

*M*eanwhile, in the kitchen

Most of the servants were already assembled around the wood plank dining table when Tom joined them for the evening meal. Despite having eaten only the hour before, he knew he would enjoy the camaraderie of the Ritchfield staff. Besides, after washing and changing into dry clothes, he was anxious to see Anne.

"Ah, look who's back in residence," Perkins said, rushing into the kitchen, his comment directed to Tom. "I have time for a quick bite 'afore I have to get back to the dining room," he added, taking one of the remaining seats at the table.

"You left the earl and countess without a servant?" Christina asked with concern.

"Served 'em soup and then their dinner, refilled their glasses, and then her ladyship waved me away," he said with a shrug. "I would have liked to have been a fly on the wall, but I can't hear a word they're saying," he added. "They're sitting right next to each other."

While Perkins spoke, Tom's attention went to Anne, who

was sitting on the opposite side of the table but nearly all the way at the other end.

She gave him a grin as he took the only remaining seat on his side of the table, and the servants he hadn't yet seen earlier that day welcomed his return.

He nodded as he glanced around to see so many familiar faces. "It's good to be back," he said. "Am I to understand his lordship is in residence?"

"He is," Graves acknowledged, the butler taking the chair at the head of the table. "Showed up yesterday during a break in the snowfall. Quite unexpectedly."

Tom leaned forward to glance down the table, his brows furrowing when he didn't see Ferguson, the earl's driver. "So where is his coach and driver?" Tom asked, remembering there wasn't a coach in the carriage house when he and Bobby had put away the countess' traveling coach.

"Ferguson went on to Wakefield with it," Graves replied. "He has some deliveries to make at one of the coal mine offices for his lordship. Apparently the heir is there now overseeing part of the earldom's business," he added, referring to Michael, the oldest son of the earl and countess. "Then Ferguson plans to spend Christmas with his family, so I don't expect him back here for a few days."

"I hope he made it there before the weather worsened," Tom commented.

"Yesterday wasn't so bad," Graves said. "Gave Mr. Ashton and Perkins a chance to cut some greens and haul them into the stable."

"I saw them," Tom said. "Or rather smelled them."

"Which brings up a good point," Graves said, clearing his throat until the conversations at the other end of the table ceased. "For those of you who were doing your jobs earlier today, you may not have been aware that the Countess Ritchfield has arrived."

From the few gasps around the table, it seemed the butler's announcement was indeed news to some. "Salisbury will be acting as her lady's maid whilst she's in residence. As is Lady Ritchfield's custom, she'll be staying until after the Twelfth Night ceremony. I don't yet have word from Lord Ritchfield as to his departure date, so everyone be on their very best behavior, and you might find something extra in your Christmas box."

A chorus of cheers sounded.

"Tomorrow is Christmas Eve, and with her ladyship here, it means we'll be spending the day decorating the house." He said this last with a pained expression on his face. "After breakfast, everyone plan to help haul in the greens from the stable and then Perkins..."

"Sir?"

"You'll bring down the trunk of supplies from the attic."

"Yes, sir."

"We'll need the men to bring in the Yule log for the main hall fireplace." A few nodded in acknowledgement. "And the rest of you can work on wiring wreaths and sprays while..." he waved a hand in a circle, "... the women make the bows and fripperies and such."

Christina giggled as two of the other maids leaned back and made faces at each other.

"The countess will be in charge, of course, so if you have any questions about where your creations should go, please ask her and not me," Graves went on.

A round of chuckling followed his comment before he added, "As she always does, Clara will make us all an early dinner, and then apparently we'll have music and dancing afterwards."

His comment resulted in a cacophony of voices, most sounding pleased with the schedule. He held up a hand to restore order. "Given the weather, I rather doubt we'll make it to church on Christmas day, but I have word from his lordship that the chapel will be available for you to use." He looked at Christina. "Mrs. Ashton, you see to cleaning the chapel, do you not?"

"I do, and I finished in there this morning," she said.

"What about Boxing Day?" one of the other maids asked.

Graves lifted a shoulder, but it was Tom who said, "I'll see to getting as many of us to Castleford as I can in her ladyship's coach," he offered.

"I can take a couple on the gig," Bobby offered.

"That leaves one horse and the phaeton," Tom commented.

"I can drive it," Perkins said. "But there will only be room for one other person up on the seat with me."

"And me on the back," one of the housemaids said with a wave, as if she had done it in the past.

There was a round of laughter before Graves said, "I have nothing else." He took his seat as the servants returned their attentions to their food and Perkins left to return to the dining room.

When the meal was complete, Tom helped to clear away dishes until he caught Anne's attention.

"Where do I meet you?" he asked in a whisper.

"The apartment closest to the drawing room," she whispered.

He nodded his understanding. "Half hour?"

She lifted a shoulder. "Depends on her ladyship."

Glancing around to be sure they weren't noticed, he said, "If I fall asleep while waiting, be sure to wake me when you come in."

Anne gave him a quelling glance until she noticed his teasing grin. She headed up the servants' stairs and a few minutes later, Tom did the same.

CHAPTER 10
QUIET LOVERS IN THE NIGHT

A half-hour later

Making his way down the servants' stairs as quietly as he could, Tom emerged into the first floor corridor, the candle lamp he held turned down so it only provided enough light to see a few steps in front of him.

The Aubusson carpet covering the wooden floor helped to drown his footfalls as he made his way past the door to the first apartment. On the other side of the next door, a lit sconce marked the entrance to the library, and he soon realized there was light coming from inside the room as well as from the sconce.

The library door was open.

Which meant someone was in the library.

He held his breath as he sneaked past and ducked into the drawing room across the hall. When he was sure he hadn't been noticed, he moved to the next door—the apartment Anne mentioned—and pushed down on the door handle until he heard the faint *snick* of the latch releasing.

Pushing on the door, Tom kept his hand on the edge of the carved wood panel until he was all the way into the apartment. He was careful to hold down the door handle until he was sure the panel was back in place before allowing it to latch.

With the help of his candle lamp, Tom could make his way through what appeared to be a salon. Without tripping over the furnishings, he made it to the only other door to discover it was open. Beyond it, another lit candle lamp was sitting on a nightstand.

No one was in the bedchamber, though, and given a fire hadn't been set in the fireplace, it was chilly.

Relieved to find several pieces of wood in a cradle next to the hearth—he knew he shouldn't be surprised since it was Anne who saw to the apartment—he went about starting a fire. The fledgling flame had barely caught the kindling when he realized he wasn't alone.

"Thank you for doing that," Anne whispered, turning to close the bedchamber door.

"Are you already finished with the countess?" Tom asked, surprised to see her so soon.

"I am. She only had me undo her hair and help with her gown," she explained, sounding confused.

"Probably because she knew you had other plans," Tom said, arching a brow.

She grinned. "I hadn't thought of that," she admitted.

"Did any of the other servants see you?"

"I didn't bother going upstairs. They all knew I would be with her ladyship this evening, but still, I made sure to come here by way of the main stairs."

Tom took her hand in his. "I think his lordship is in the library."

"He is," she agreed. "Graves set a fire for him right after dinner."

Glancing around the bedchamber, Tom noticed she had already turned down the bed. "I haven't been in a bed this size since..." He allowed the sentence to trail off lest he mention his late wife.

"Never for me," she said, moving to sit on the edge of it. She gave it an experimental bounce. "The ropes are tight," she murmured.

He joined her there, wrapping an arm around the back of her shoulders to pull her to him. "When I left you last year—after you kissed me so sweetly whilst I stood next to the coach—I was thinking about you all the way to London. Then you wrote to me so often—"

"And you wrote back," she whispered.

"—I promised myself I wasn't going to ever leave you again. That is, if you still felt the same way now as you did then."

"I do," she whispered.

He chuckled softly. "I wasn't sure until you found me on the stairs earlier."

She dipped her head as a blush appeared. "You probably thought me fast."

"The thought didn't cross my mind," he countered. "It only convinced me of the words in your letters." He turned to face her. "I meant what I said about not leaving you," he warned. "When I take her ladyship back to London after Twelfth Night, you're coming with us."

She nodded, her grin widening into a smile. "I know. She told me."

Tom gave a start. "What's this?" Although he knew Lady Ritchfield was aware he was sweet on Anne—she had given him a number of missives from Anne over the past year even though the butler probably should have been the one to do so—he had never talked to her about his intentions toward the housemaid.

"She wants me to be her lady's maid. In London," Anne said, lifting a hand to the side of his neck.

His gaze going to his mind's eye, Tom chuckled softly. "She's finally going to pension that old goat," he whispered.

"What's this?"

Shaking his head, he turned his gaze back on her. "Watkins. Her lady's maid. Probably a hundred years old and not a very nice woman, if you ask me. A more stubborn woman you won't find anywhere else," he murmured. "You'll be a welcome addition to the staff, I should think."

Anne regarded him with a grin. "Does the rest of the staff there know? About us, I mean?"

His look of confusion quickly passed. "Not yet, but they will," he said. "Because I'm going to introduce you as me wife," he claimed.

Her eyes widened. "Oh, are you now?"

Stiffening, he said, "I am." When he realized what she meant, he scoffed. "Well, you are going to marry me, aren't you? Because..." he turned and waved a hand at the bed. "We're not spending the night in the same bed if you're not."

Anne sighed and tried her best to keep a straight face. "Well, if that's the best you can do for a marriage proposal, then I suppose I have to accept it," she chided.

Tom inhaled to answer before his brows furrowed. "Oh, that didn't come out how I was expectin' to do it," he admitted. "My apologies." He stood from the bed and turned to face her. Lifting her hands, one in each of his, he said, "Miss Salisbury, will you do me the honor of becoming me wife?"

Anne grinned and nodded. "I will, Mr. Walker."

The two stared at one another for a long time before he gathered her into his arms and kissed her.

He had the ties of her apron undone and the buttons unfastened at the top of her livery before their lips separated. When he glanced down, he discovered she had already unbuttoned his waistcoat.

He pulled off her apron and was about to lift her gown when he paused. "Should I put you into bed first? It's still a bit chilly in here," he whispered.

"I hadn't noticed," she murmured, pushing his waistcoat from his body. She was undoing the knot in his cravat when he wrapped his hands around her wrists.

"Have you seen a man before? Without clothes on, I mean?"

Understanding immediately what he was asking, she lifted her gaze to meet his. "In paintings, I suppose," she replied.

"Because I don't know what you're expecting, but—"

"I don't know what you're expecting, either," she interrupted, shaking her wrists free of his hold so she could continue undoing his cravat. "But we'll turn down the candle lamps so it will be dark—"

"But I want to see you," he argued.

Anne stilled her hands. "Do you mean, in my shift, or...?"

"Well, the *or*," he affirmed. When he heard her scoff of shock, he added, "I know you'll be gorgeous, Anne. Much finer looking than me, that's for certain."

She draped his cravat over the back of a chair and extinguished the candle lamp she had brought as well as the other two. The flames in the fireplace, now spread over all the logs, cast more than enough light in the room.

"If you insist, but I'm leaving my stockings on," she stated. She encouraged him to sit on the bed so she could pull his boots from his feet. "I better not see a single look of disappointment, though." The first boot landed with a thud a few feet away.

"You won't," he agreed. "But I'm keeping my shirt on. To be sure I won't see a look of disappointment from you."

She scoffed. "It's hardly the same," she said, tossing his second boot to land atop the first. Coming to her feet, she reached for the sides of his shirt and began pulling the fabric from his breeches.

"Have you done this before?" he asked, his voice barely a whisper.

Beneath the hem of his shirt, she had her hand on one of the buttons of his breeches, and she stilled. "No," she replied. "Of course not."

He exhaled a breath he didn't know he had been holding. "You've never...?"

Resuming her work on undoing the buttons, she shook her head. "I've not been with a man before, if that's what you're asking." She palmed the hard ridge that had formed behind the placket of his breeches. "But I know what happens between a man and a woman. I'm not some young girl fresh from the schoolroom."

Tom squeezed his eyes shut when he felt her hand press against his manhood. He had hoped to retain some control—this was their first time together like this—but if she continued what she was doing, he would be coming far sooner than he planned.

"Anne, I really need you to stop that," he whispered. He placed a hand over hers to move it aside, and he felt how it trembled in his hold.

"Did I hurt you?" she asked in confusion.

He shook his head. "Anything but," he replied. "However, I don't want to hurt *you*, so we're going to take our time, and I'm going to be sure you're as ready for me as I am for you."

She nodded and watched as he pushed his breeches and smalls from his body, followed by his stockings. The entire time, his shirt hid his manhood from sight.

He knelt before her and removed her shoes, and as he stood, supporting himself by gripping the poster at the end of the bed, he brought up the hem of her gown with his other hand. She didn't put voice to a protest but raised her arms as he pulled the black gown over her head.

He was careful to shake it out and drape it over the same chair where she had left his clothes so neatly folded. When he faced her once again, he undid her stays and pulled them from her body.

Her white cotton shift hung down past the tops of her stockings, the thin fabric doing nothing to hide the tips of her nipples or the dark triangle at the top of her thighs.

Tom swallowed. "See? You are gorgeous," he whispered.

Anne stepped close enough so the fronts of their bodies touched. "I'm not sure if you are aware, but you're standing in front of the fire," she said, arching a teasing brow.

He chuckled. "So you think you've seen everything," he guessed.

She nodded.

He stripped the shift from her body, turned and lifted her into his arms, Anne letting out a squeak of surprise as she gripped his shoulder. "Mr. Walker!" she scolded.

He merely grinned as he took her to the bed and placed her in the middle, his gaze on her face the entire time. Hearing her soft gasp when her bare skin touched the cool bed linens, he quickly moved to pull up some of the blankets to cover her, then climbed in behind her, doffing his shirt at the last minute. Gathering her into his arms, he kissed her with an urgency matching how she had kissed him in the stairwell. Despite their combined warmth, he still felt her trembling.

"What do I do?" she asked, when he finally ended the kiss.

"Allow me," he said, his lips working their way down her cheek and to the space between her neck and shoulder. "To do this," he added in a whisper.

She inhaled sharply at the sensation of his suckling lips, of his warm hand as it smoothed over her skin and cupped a breast to gently mold it. By then, he had his mouth there, too, his lips taking purchase on her nipple to worry it with his tongue and teeth.

When he turned his attention to the other breast, Anne had moved a hand to his head, her fingers spearing his hair and her nails scraping his scalp. Frissons skittered down his spine, and he had to let go of the nipple to inhale sharply. "You minx," he accused.

Anne tittered, gripping his head with both hands. He wasn't about to be deterred from his mission, though. Sliding down her body, he kissed her belly and then blew on the moisture left behind. Hearing her soft gasps only encouraged him. His tongue darted into her naval as he used a hand to push one of her thighs to the side.

When he moved lower, she bent her other leg, her breaths becoming louder. "What...?"

"Ssh," he replied, his lips skimming over the tender skin of her inner thigh.

He felt her buck beneath him, but he wasn't about to stop, not when his tongue was so close to its target.

He had his arms beneath her knees and his hands spread on her thighs when he glanced up her body. Although he knew she had been trying to watch what he was doing, he saw how her back had arched and her chest was raised. She had the bed linens gripped in her hands, her head tilted back on the pillow.

"Breathe, my sweet," he said, right before his tongue slid between the folds covering her womanhood. He wasn't expecting her to already be wet with need, but he knew she was even before he slid his tongue over the swollen nubbin. Circling it with his tongue several times, he listened to her quiet mewls and felt her lower body quake beneath his chin.

Sliding his tongue deep into her warm channel, he thrilled when he felt her body respond, the waves of her orgasm attempting to pull him in deeper. Desperate for his own release, he was up and over her in an instant, his manhood at her entrance. He pushed into her before she had a chance to realize what he was doing, before she had a chance to clench in an attempt to prevent his entry.

"Oh!"

"Breathe," he said again, his mouth covering hers with a kiss. When he lifted his head from hers, he asked, "Are you all right?"

Her gaze darted about for a moment before she nodded in the pillow. "I... I think so."

When he slowly pulled almost all the way out of her, she moved her hands on his shoulders. "What...?"

He slid a warm hand along her side, his thumb brushing the side of her breast. "Hang on to me," he whispered. He pushed back into her, this time until he was as deep as he could go.

Anne inhaled slowly, nodding in the pillow even as she lifted her knees so they gripped his thighs.

Tom groaned his appreciation, resuming the retreat and thrusting motions of a dance as ancient as time. On his fourth thrust, Anne lifted her hips to meet his, and it was nearly his undoing. "Oh, my sweet, I do love you," he whispered, his breathing ragged as he continued the movements that soon had him holding his breath and his body seizing as his orgasm gripped him in pure pleasure.

Anne slid her hands from his shoulders as his arms seemed to lose all their strength. When he nearly fell onto her, his chest pressed to hers, she wrapped her arms around his back and held on as he rolled onto his back.

Not letting go, Anne gasped, her eyes wide as she stared down at him. "Are you all right?"

He chuckled softly when he realized she had held onto him, her thighs still gripping his, her chest against his, her gaze one of concern.

Nodding, he said, "Better than I have been in my entire life, my love. And you?" His slid his hands up and down her sides, well aware her body still trembled.

She managed a wan grin. "Will we do it again?"

His eyes rounded. "Tonight?"

Blinking, she was hesitant with her nod.

Chuckling again, he seemed to think on it a moment before he said, "Well, mayhap in the morning, before we... before we have to leave this wonderful bed?" he countered.

She nodded. "All right. May I stay where I am?" She straightened her legs, wincing when his manhood left her body.

Grinning, he lifted his head to kiss her on the lips. "For the entire night if you'd like." He watched as she reached around to pull the bed linens over their bodies and settle her head onto his chest. Kissing her on the top of her head, he whispered, "Good night, my love," and promptly fell asleep.

*A*top him, Anne wondered how he could sleep. Her entire body seemed to buzz with excitement, her nerve endings behaving as if they had been asleep her entire life. She was aware of every thread in the bed linens and of the warm body below, of his pulse beneath her ear and the way it caused a tremor in his chest with every heartbeat. Of the scent of woodsmoke from the fireplace and the quiet crackles as the fire consumed the logs. Of the sounds of the house as the rooms cooled with the winter chill beyond the outer walls.

Eventually, she fell asleep, her last thought that she was betrothed to be married and would soon be moving to London.

CHAPTER 11
LONELY NO MORE

*M*eanwhile, in the library

With the flames in the fireplace barely licking the last of the logs, Robert Strathford raised his gaze from an old book and allowed a sigh. His glass of brandy had been empty for nearly an hour, but he had no desire for another. He felt tired enough to sleep, but the events of the day had his mind in a whirl.

Ivy had his mind in a whirl.

Their dinner hadn't been the least bit awkward—not like they usually were when he returned to London for the Season. She was the one who was comfortable and in charge there, the servants loyal to her, and she in her element as a countess in good standing with the ladies of the *ton*. He always felt like an intruder, as if his mere presence upset the daily life of the townhouse in Mayfair.

Here at Ritchfield Park, things were obviously different. The servants hadn't expected either one of them to come for Christmas, and although they did his bidding, they seemed devoted to her.

Probably because she brings them presents, he considered on a sigh. Then he chided himself for the uncharitable thought.

Would she have one for him? He rolled his eyes at the reminder he didn't have one for her. Once again, the holiday had sneaked up on him, and he hadn't the time to have something made for her.

He stood from the leather chair and stretched, his attention going to the door at the opposite end of the room. Earlier that evening, he had been aware of movement out in the corridor. Not because he heard anything exactly, but more likely because he had felt it in the floorboards. Careful steps. Like those of a servant not wishing to disturb the master of the house.

Then he remembered Ivy's comment over dinner. That she had given her new lady's maid permission to use one of the apartments on the first floor.

On this floor.

Robert blew out the candle lamp he had been using to light the pages of his book and made his way to the library door. Somewhere nearby, a couple was in bed and engaged in who knew what manner of lovemaking, no doubt warm and cozy in each other's arms.

A glance at the clock on the mantel had him amending his thought—they were probably sound asleep given how early they rose in the morning. Still, the jealousy he experienced— he would be going to a cold bed while they were warm in each other's arms—bothered him.

Climbing the stairs to the second floor, he had a thought to simply join Ivy in her bedchamber.

Would she put voice to a protest?

He paused in front of her door.

Given how she had looked at him when he bade her goodnight earlier, he didn't think she would. But with tomorrow's schedule—he could imagine how involved she would be with decorating the house for Christmas—he moved on to his bedchamber door and went in.

The room was warm, the fire still strong in the fireplace, but no candle lamps were lit near the bed. In the dim light, he thought it odd the bedding hadn't been turned down, the silhouettes of several decorative pillows evident in the gloom.

Having dismissed Graves earlier by saying he could undress himself, Robert did so now. He undid buttons and fastenings and draped his clothes over chairs as he removed each article. Given how cold he expected the room to be in the morning, he pulled on a night shirt and moved to the side of the bed.

About to climb in, he paused and leaned down closer to discover the lumps he had assumed were pillows were actually a body.

Under the covers.

Ivy?

He gingerly pulled back the covers and slipped into the bed linens, a soft chuckle sounding when he realized it was indeed Ivy. She wasn't naked, but she wasn't wearing a night rail, either, her gown's fabric soft and slippery. Her even breathing was a sign she was asleep.

Before he was completely settled on the mattress, she snuggled against him, one leg moving between his and an arm draping onto his chest as he threaded an arm beneath her shoulders and pulled her closer.

He realized her coppery hair wasn't bound into a braid when waves of it settled onto his chest. Tipping up his head, he planted a kiss atop hers and settled into the pillow with a sigh.

He needn't have worried about climbing into a cold bed. Ivy's body was soft and warm, and although he had a last thought about what he'd like to be doing with that body to create even more warmth, he was soon fast asleep.

CHAPTER 12
CHRISTMAS EVE MORNING

The following morning in the breakfast parlor

"Good morning, Ritchfield," Ivy said brightly, appearing on the threshold of the breakfast parlor wearing a festive day gown. Her coppery hair was styled in a riot of curls atop her head while one wavy lock rested over a shoulder.

"Happy Christmas Eve," Robert said, looking up from a newspaper and then quickly standing. From the few items remaining on his plate, it was apparent he had already eaten. "You were up early this morning," he added, moving to hold her chair for her.

He had awakened to discover he was alone, although the bed was still warm where her body had been. The reminder of her had his morning tumescence tenting the bed linens longer than usual, so it had been almost a relief when Graves appeared to help him dress.

"I always am on Christmas Eve," she replied, her grin widening into a smile. "Hanging of the greens." She watched as he retook his seat. "You were up terribly late last night. I hope all is well?"

Robert leaned back in his chair and crossed his arms. "I was reading in the library," he said.

Perkins appeared and placed a salver bearing a small teapot, cup, saucer, and sugar-pot before her and refilled Robert's coffee cup from a pitcher already on the table.

"What has Clara made this morning?" Ivy asked turning her attention on the servant.

"Almost anything you want, my lady," he replied. "She cooked a feast for us servants this morn."

"Then I'll have toast, coddled eggs, and bacon," she said.

"I'll bring them right away, my lady." He turned to Robert. "Would you like anything else, my lord?"

Robert unfolded his arms and straightened in his chair. "I'd like an orange," he said.

Perkins' eyes rounded. "Yes, my lord."

From the other side of the table, Ivy blinked. "Those are supposed to be for later," she scolded.

"I heard you brought an entire crate of them with you," he countered.

She grinned. "I did. Two of them."

"And that I'll be receiving an invoice for them," he added, smirking.

Tittering, Ivy prepared her tea. "This is one of my favorite days of the year," she said. "I adore how everything looks when we finish with all the greenery. So festive. And the entire house smells so good for an entire fortnight," she gushed.

"I thought I smelled pine when Graves opened my door this morning," he murmured.

"I'm sure you did if the servants have started bringing them in," she said with excitement. "The Yule log, too," she added, her eyes widening at seeing the breakfast Perkins set before her. "Oh, it's a veritable feast."

"As was mine," Robert remarked.

"Will you help with the greenery?" she asked, before taking a sip of tea. "The sooner we're done, the sooner we can have an early dinner and begin the dancing in the great hall."

Robert angled his head to one side as he watched her tuck into her breakfast. "Dancing?" he repeated.

"You don't have to dance, but the servants will want to. This is one of those festive evenings," she insisted.

"I thought that was supposed to be the Twelfth Night," he said in confusion.

"It is, darling, but we celebrate Christmas Eve here as well," she explained.

His eyes widened when Perkins set a peeled orange before him, the sections splayed out to make it look as if it was a flower with orange petals. "If there's dancing, then who provides the music?" he asked, using a fork to retrieve one of the orange sections.

She lifted a shoulder. "Well, I'll play the piano-forté and Mr. Ashton, the groom, will play his violin," she replied. When he simply stared at her, she sighed softly. "You've never done this before, have you?" she teased.

"Apparently not," he replied, experimentally tasting the orange. "But I'm willing to try."

Ivy beamed in delight before tucking into her breakfast.

"Did your lady's maid happen to mention how her evening went last night?" he asked in a quiet voice. "I'm fairly sure she took advantage of your most generous offer of the apartment," he added, his brow arching.

Her eyes rounding, Ivy said, "Oh, dear. Did they disturb you whilst you were in the library?'

Shaking his head, Robert chuckled softly. "I did not hear them, if that's what you're asking." He almost said something about how jealous he had felt knowing the servants were engaged in lovemaking while he would have liked to have been doing the same thing with his wife. Had he simply gone to bed when he bid Ivy good-night, he might have been doing the same thing.

"Well, I'm glad to hear it because Salisbury gave me the most wonderful news this morning when she was doing my hair."

"Which is rather lovely," Robert remarked, surprised when he saw a blush color her face.

"Oh, thank you for saying so," she replied, her fingers stroking the lock of hair that hung down in front of one shoulder. "It's probably too daring for London, but we're in the country—"

"You should have her style it like that more often," he said, "Hang London."

"Ritchfield," she scolded, despite the grin she displayed. "Well, I'm glad you like it because I have decided I am going to take her back to London with me to be my lady's maid."

Robert furrowed a brow, sure there was more to it, but her comment reminded him of their conversation at dinner the night before. "So she accepted your offer of employment?"

"I made mention of it, and she seemed quite pleased with the prospect. But I haven't made her a formal offer," she explained.

"Mayhap you could bring her with you to York first."

Ivy inhaled softly. "Perhaps," she murmured. "I was going to see to the final arrangements for Watkins' dismissal—"

"I can see to it with a letter to your butler and my man of business," he interrupted.

"I didn't bring many gowns with me—"

"We can have her pack up some more of your clothes and have them sent to the house in York," he suggested. "*Before* the butler speaks with her."

Ivy considered his words before she finally nodded. "All right," she agreed before her eyes widened. "Oh, I'll have to let Walker know, what with *his* new situation."

"Your driver?"

Ivy's eyes rounded. "Oh, I meant to tell you the good news. Mr. Walker and Miss Salisbury are to be married. He proposed last night."

Seeing the joy on his wife's face had Robert smirking even as his chest tightened. He hadn't even been in her company for an entire day, and yet he was reminded of why he had fallen in love with her in the first place.

The red hair had certainly caught his eye back then—how could it not?—the tresses the color of flames and copper in the sun. Then there had been her generous bosom, her rising moons begging to be traced and touched above the neckline of her presentation gown.

But it had been the sheer delight in her green eyes that had truly captured his attention. Whilst every other young lady seemed petrified about the prospect of being presented to the queen, she had displayed happiness.

He had seen that same expression of delight whenever something pleased her, which had his gaze seeking hers from across ballrooms and parlors, Rotten Row and the theatre.

Even after they wed, he had felt challenged to come up with gestures that would elicit the same reaction from her. The gift of a tiny bauble or a compliment on her gown, a soft kiss at the nape of her neck or an open-mouthed kiss when he returned from Parliament.

Wishing to extend her happiness over her new lady's maid's announcement, he was about to leave the breakfast table, pull her up from her chair and kiss her senseless, but Graves appeared at the door.

"Pardon me, my lady, but you asked to be informed about the status of the greenery?"

"Yes, Graves. How goes it?"

"The servants have brought everything into the house, and the Yule log is in place on the hearth in the hall," he stated.

"Perkins has the work table set up in the hall and the trunk brought down from the attic. I believe we are ready to begin, my lady."

Although he wasn't so sure his kiss would have been as welcome as Graves' announcement, Robert couldn't be too upset when Ivy stood from her chair and displayed an expression of infectious delight.

"Oh, we can start now," she gushed. She turned her gaze on Robert and said, "Are you coming?"

Tempted to make an excuse—he could hide in his study or the library—Robert stood and took a deep breath. "If you think I'll be of any assistance, then, I suppose I will join you."

He was more surprised than Graves when she rushed over to him and kissed him on the cheek. "You'll want to wear some old gloves, Ritchfield. To keep the sap off your fingers," she said, hooking her arm into his. "They'll be in the trunk that Perkins has brought down. And do be careful whilst you're doing the wiring. The ends are always rather sharp, and I don't want you impaling yourself."

"I appreciate that," Robert replied, giving Graves a beseeching glance as they made their way out of the breakfast parlor and to the workroom at the back of the house.

Usually used by the servants when they were mending, ironing, or folding clothes, the room had been transformed on this day by the addition of a wheelbarrow filled with greenery. Several cutting tools and rounds of wire were scattered about the trestle centered in the room along with gloves of various sizes. "This is where the sprays and wreaths are wired together," Ivy explained. "The housemaids are working at the servants' table in the kitchen."

"What are they making?"

"The bows and other decorations, of course," she replied. "Oh, and don't forget to make a kissing bough, if you would. We didn't have one last year."

"I can't imagine why," Robert deadpanned.

She gave him a quelling glance. "There's no mistletoe to be found around these parts, so we must make do," she explained.

"And how, pray tell, is a kissing bough supposed to look?" he asked, helping himself to a pair of gloves. He experimentally fisted and opened his hand to determine they were a good fit.

"You really don't do this at Gladstone Hall?" she asked.

"*I* do not. The servants see to it," he replied defensively.

"Well, it's a small evergreen bough, so you needn't use a lot of greenery. Just form it into a sort of ball and the maids will see to adding paper flowers and apples—"

"Apples?"

"Yes. Oh, I brought some with me," she said.

"Is there any foodstuff you didn't bring with you?" he asked rhetorically.

"Venison," she stated without a pause.

"I could maybe see to bagging a stag whilst I'm here," he offered. "In fact..." He was about to remove the gloves when Ivy placed a hand on his arm.

"It's far too cold out there, darling," she whispered, gently squeezing his arm. "Perhaps when it warms up. After Christmas," she added.

"Oh, all right," he said, pulling the glove back on. "So what else is going to be attached to this kissing bough? It sounds as if I need to make it big enough so there is room for all the fripperies," he said.

"Well, one year they made dolls from fabric representing Mary, Joseph, and Jesus and added those to the flowers and the apples."

Robert scrunched his face into a grimace. "And where exactly does this kissing bough get hung?"

Ivy lifted a shoulder. "In a doorway somewhere. Perkins

will see to it. I'll be sure to lead you there at some point," she added with a wink.

She didn't bother to mention that last year, Perkins had hung the kissing bough over the entry to the kitchen and then insisted he be kissed every time a maid had to make her way through the door.

Although it had led to the fallout betwixt Perkins and Graves—Graves had not been amused by the footman's antics—it had resulted in the marriage of the groom, Bobby, to the housemaid, Christina.

*R*obert had to resist the urge to counter Ivy's wink with one of his own. "I shall do my best, my lady," he said, shoo'ing her out of the workroom.

What had he gotten himself into?

CHAPTER 13
DECORATING ON CHRISTMAS EVE

A few minutes later

Satisfied her husband couldn't hurt himself too badly with his assignment, Ivy made her way to the kitchen and stopped short on the threshold.

Lengths of red fabric had been cut and were in the process of being formed into massive bows by some of the maids while others were tying them onto wreaths and sprays with yarn. When the largest was complete, Perkins climbed a ladder and saw to mounting it above the fireplace in the great hall. Another was already nailed to the front door.

At noon, Barbara, the scullery maid, appeared with trays of small pasties and scones, and she was followed by Clara, who carried a large tea service. Behind them, Graves wheeled over a cart with plates and cups. Anne appeared carrying a platter on which a colorful collection of fruits was arranged. On closer inspection, Ivy realized they weren't fruits, but rather decorations made of marchpane.

Before long, the men from the workroom joined the women and quieted as they ate and drank. A half-hour later, they were back at it, making decorations and long garlands for the bannisters.

Ivy inhaled deeply upon entering the parlor, the scent of pine wafting about from above the fireplace. "Oh, Salisbury, I do think it's perfect," she said, admiring the spray the housemaid had placed on the fireplace mantel. The maid was tying a red ribbon bow in the middle and arranging the evergreens so they weren't in danger of catching fire.

Anne dipped a curtsy and beamed in delight. "This is my favorite time of year, and not only because Mr. Walker has asked me for my hand," she replied.

Sighing softly, Ivy said, "I'm so happy for you. Have you told the others?"

"Not yet. I thought Mr. Walker might say something at breakfast this morning, but he didn't have a chance, what with all the chatter about what we were going to be doing today," Anne said. "I've never worked in a household that did this much decorating for the holiday."

Ivy grinned. "It's my favorite time of the year as well, more so when my children were younger." She moved to one of the windows and peered out through the frosted glass pane. A world of white lay beyond, the snow pristine and glistening as if silver glitter had been scattered over it. "Would it be all right if his lordship announced your betrothal, do you suppose?"

Anne inhaled softly. "I suppose, although I think it's really Mr. Walker's decision."

"Well, then let's go find him and ask."

On the way down the stairs, they stepped around Perkins, who was wrapping garlands around the bannister. In the kitchens, the cook was preparing that night's meal featuring the ham she had brought from London.

"I did not expect his lordship to help with all this," Salisbury said, waving to the string of evergreens. "He seemed so eager to assist, and I do believe he's better at the wiring than Perkins." She directed a teasing grin at the footman, and rather than deny it, he merely shrugged.

Ivy tittered. "Ritchfield is full of surprises," she murmured, arching a brow when she felt a frisson skitter through her abdomen. The way he had gazed at her during breakfast, she was sure he was imagining doing something entirely different on this day. Something involving a bed and very little in the way of clothing.

"I admit I was rather frightened of him at first, my lady," Salisbury said, turning to face Ivy. "I had never met his lordship before last night. It's why I left your bedchamber before you… before you had a chance to dismiss me," she said sheepishly.

"He noticed. Said he thought you were a bit skittish," she remarked as they made their way to the workroom. "Which reminds me. I've been invited to join his lordship in York after the holiday. Since we've decided it's past time I pension my lady's maid in London, I wondered if you might like the position? Permanently?"

The housemaid's eyes rounded. "Me?" she asked in surprise. "Why, yes. Yes, I would like it very much, my lady," she added. "Especially since I've agreed to marry Mr. Walker."

Ivy sobered. "You would be leaving this household, at least until the next time I come back. Probably…" She thought for a moment. "In the summer, perhaps."

"I don't mind," Anne insisted.

"You have no family here who would miss you?" the countess asked. "In Castleford or Wakefield?"

"I don't have any family, my lady," the maid replied, shaking her head to emphasize her words. "Well, except for Mr. Walker once we're wed. And I do so enjoy styling your hair."

Ivy grinned. "Good, because Ritchfield rather likes what you've done with it, and I do believe it's the first time in thirty years he's even noticed my coiffure." She angled her head. "There are other duties regarding my clothes and such, but we can talk more about that later."

Anne blushed. "Thank you, my lady. For the opportunity," she said, dipping a curtsy.

They found both Walker and the earl in the workroom, each wiring a series of pine boughs into long sections. "Ah," Ivy said, turning to shut the door. "We've found you."

Robert looked up from his project and immediately stood, followed by Tom, who bowed.

"Should I be worried?" Robert asked. He had removed his top coat, and his sleeves were rolled up to his elbows. His hands, encased in leather gloves, held a pair of shears to cut thin wire into sections about a foot long.

"Nothing of the sort. We only wished to ask Mr. Walker if it would be all right with him if you announced his betrothal to Miss Salisbury?"

Robert turned his attention on the driver. "Did you propose marriage to Miss Salisbury?"

Tom straightened, obviously not expecting such a query. "I did, my lord. Last night, and she accepted," he replied.

"Have you told the staff yet?"

"No, my lord," Tom admitted. "I thought to during breakfast, but everyone was so excited about decorating the house."

"Well, if you'd like, I can do it. I'm quite sure her ladyship has something planned for me later this afternoon?" Robert guessed, aiming an inquisitive expression in Ivy's direction.

"I'd like that, my lord," Tom acknowledged. "If we have your blessing."

Robert gave a start, as if he hadn't considered the

repercussions of their marriage. He once again directed his gaze to Ivy. "Ritchfield Park is going to lose a housemaid," he murmured.

"It was going to lose her anyway," Ivy said. "Miss Salisbury has accepted my offer to become my new lady's maid," she explained. "If he goes to Castleford on Boxing Day, I'm quite sure Graves can post the position. It will no doubt be filled before you leave for York."

A wince showed on Robert's face, but only for an instant before it cleared. He turned to Tom. "You have my blessing."

"Thank you, my lord." Tom exhibited a look of relief and then directed a grin in Anne's direction.

"Do what you must to keep her happy," Robert stated.

"I will, my lord."

"Never strike her in anger or raise your voice to her," Robert went on. "Or I'll see to it you never see her again."

Tom's eyes rounded. "No, my lord," he replied, a look of alarm appearing. "I would never hit a woman, my lord."

Robert inhaled and held the breath for a moment before letting it out. "Very good." He stripped his gloves from his hands. "I'll be in my study," he said before he suddenly took his leave.

Ivy watched him go, a brow furrowed with worry. The earl's last directives had been entirely unexpected, as had his departure. Turning to Tom, she asked, "Will you be able to finish what his lordship started?"

Tom regarded the pile of wires the earl had already cut. "It appears his lordship has cut enough wire to make a dozen more wreaths, my lady, so I shall continue making garlands for the stairs."

Allowing a wan grin, Ivy nodded. She turned to Anne. "Come. Let's go see what trouble the men have gotten themselves into with the Yule log." She really wanted to go to the study to speak with her husband, but thought to give him a few minutes alone.

"Yes, my lady."

They paused as they passed the bottom of the stairs, Ivy giving Perkins a reassuring nod when she saw that he was nearly done with wrapping pine boughs around one of the railings. "It appears we're going to need more bows for the stairs."

"I can do it, my lady," Anne offered. She dipped a curtsy and hurried off toward the kitchen where two other maids were busy with tying bows to greenery.

Surveying the great hall, Ivy couldn't help but allow a sigh of satisfaction at finding a bright fire crackling in the fireplace. A length of greenery had been draped over the entire width of the mantel, and in front of the fireplace, a massive log lay resting on the hearth. She immediately moved to sit on it, grinning as she did so.

"Whatever are you doing?"

She looked up to see Robert leaning against the door jamb of the study, a look of amusement on his face. "Sitting on the Yule log. For good luck," she replied. "I take it you don't do this at Gladstone Hall any longer?"

He looked suitably chagrined. "The servants do, I'm sure," he said before joining her to sit on the log. "Are we to light it now?"

Ivy noted how the work table that had been set up in the hall was now abandoned, the cuttings from the pine boughs and resulting needles now cleaned away. "We should probably wait until we can gather everyone together," she said. "So they have a chance to sit on the log, too."

"So... this isn't a private affair?" he asked in a whisper.

A frisson skittered beneath Ivy's skin, and she glanced about as if she was sure someone had paid witness to it.

"Unfortunately, no. The entire household should be here to witness it since it's a sign of good luck and good health." When she saw he was about to bark an order, she placed a hand on his arm. "Thank you for giving Walker your blessing," she whispered.

Robert stilled and turned to regard her with furrowed brows. "I wasn't about to deny him," he replied. "He has a second chance at life with a woman for whom he obviously cares a great deal."

Awestruck at hearing the comment, Ivy's mouth dropped open. "And yet the recommendations you made to him were rather... odd. Is everything all right?"

Stiffening, Robert regarded her with an expression of regret. "I think those ghosts we talked about last night might have had some influence on what I said," he admitted.

"Robert," she whispered softly. "What's happened. What haven't you told me?"

He surveyed the area around him, as if he, too, was concerned they might be overheard. "I never told you about my father. What he did to my mother. How foolishly possessive he was of her," he murmured, his gaze turning to his mind's eye. "And yet, I know exactly how he felt, because I have been experiencing it with you of late."

Ivy swallowed. Although she had never met his parents—both long dead before she married Robert—she had frequently wondered why he rarely spoke of them. "You're feeling... possessive?" she asked in a quiet voice.

He nodded.

"Well, I suppose I am your property since I am your wife," she reminded him.

Giving her a quelling glance, he dipped his head. "I never thought of you like that, Ivy. But something happened at Gladstone Hall, and..." He stopped and raised his face to the ceiling.

"*What* happened, Robert?" she asked in alarm.

"I, uh..." He cleared his throat. "I nearly pummeled the butler to death," he stammered, his voice strangled.

Ivy inhaled sharply, her brows furrowing in shock. "Hartfield? But why?" was all she could think to ask.

"The housekeeper—"

"Mrs. Hartfield?"

He nodded. "Yes. She, uh, brought tea to my study... the day before I came here... and, uh, her face was all bruised. Said she fell," he added, rolling his eyes.

"Oh, dear."

"It all came back at once, Ivy. All those times I saw my mother like that." He closed his eyes and shook his head as if to clear it of the memory.

"Oh, Robert," she breathed in a whisper. "I... I had no idea. You never spoke of it."

"Of course not. I had thought it was all dead and buried with them," he murmured. "When I confronted Hartfield—I found him in his office—he acted as if he had done nothing wrong. 'The late earl did it to his wife all the time,' he told me."

Ivy swallowed, her eyes wide with fright. "He was the ghost," she whispered in awe.

Robert turned to look at her directly. "All that rage I felt... it all went into my fists," he said, holding out his hands. The scuff marks on the back of his knuckles had faded, but one was still swollen.

Even though she had noticed them the night before, Ivy's gaze dropped to study them. She lifted the one with the injured knuckle and leaned down to gently kiss it. "I'm so sorry, Robert."

"I probably would have killed him if his wife hadn't screamed for me to stop."

Tears pricked the corners of Ivy's eyes. "And then?" she prompted.

"I fired him. Told him to pack up and get out, and that if I ever so much as saw him again, I would have him flogged."

Ivy inhaled softly. "And Mrs. Hartfield?"

He gave a start. "Well, I didn't let *her* go," he said. "I told her she was under my protection, and I told her that she wasn't to go with him." He paused a moment. "Truth be told, I do think she was relieved to be rid of him."

"No doubt," she said on a sigh. "So... did Hartfield leave?"

Robert nodded. "He did. I, uh, immediately promoted the under butler, and I went and hid in my study."

"Sanderson?" she guessed.

He nodded.

"He'll do fine," she assured him.

"And that's when I reread your letters." He cleared his throat. "I wanted to be sure I had never done anything like that to you."

"Never," she whispered.

"That you hadn't stayed away because you felt *threatened* by me."

"No, Robert," she assured him.

"Because there have been times in the past few years when I have felt such frustration, I used to punch the damned pillows on my bed," he admitted. "So I joined a boxing saloon, where I can punch large bags of sand instead."

"Oh," she breathed, reaching for one of his hands to grip it in hers. "Because of something I said? Or something I did?"

"Because I *missed* you, damn it, and I didn't know what to do to get you..." He couldn't go on, not when her other hand had moved to pull his face to hers, not when her lips captured his in a kiss that had him pulling her onto his lap and continuing it as if his very life depended on it.

This time, she was sure it did.

When she finally let go to take a breath, Robert stared at her for a full second before blinking several times. "Well, I do believe this Yule log is working," he murmured.

Ivy let out a nervous titter. "Indeed," she agreed. They sat in companionable silence for a moment before she added, "Perhaps it's time we share it, though."

Robert's sigh sounded his reluctance before he finally called out, "Graves!"

The butler hurried into the hall. "My lord?" He gave a start when he saw the two of them perched on the Yule log, the countess sitting across the earl's lap.

"Have all the servants join us," Robert ordered. "I understand some consider it good luck to sit on the Yule log before it's rolled into the fireplace," he said. "Then we're going to light this log and hope it doesn't set the entire house on fire," he added with a grin.

"Yes, my lord." Graves disappeared as quickly as he had arrived.

Robert helped Ivy to stand before he rolled down his sleeves and stood. "I feel entirely underdressed," he murmured, even though he was only missing his top coat.

"You look fine, darling," she said, brushing the back of her gown with a hand before shaking out her skirts. "Do I look as if I've been tumbled?"

He let out a guffaw. "Just you wait, my lady," he said in a warning.

Ivy allowed a wobbly grin and then stood on tiptoes to kiss him again.

Robert gave a start. He would have continued to kiss her, but four maids, Perkins, the laundress, the cook and the scullery maid, a driver, and the groom had joined them in the hall. When they were finished lining up in a semi-circle, they collectively curtsied and bowed.

"If you believe in such a thing as good luck, which I do, by the way, now is your chance," Robert said, waving to the log.

He and Ivy stepped aside and watched as the servants took turns sitting on the Yule log, Tom and Anne doing so at the same time, as did Bobby and Christina. After everyone had a chance, the male servants joined forces to roll it into the fireplace, nearly extinguishing the existing fire in the process.

"Time to light it," someone said.

"Would you like to do the honors?" Robert asked, turning to Ivy. "You're far more familiar with this tradition than I am."

"Oh, I think you should do it, Ritchfield," she said, "But first you'll need the leftover piece from last year's log." She rushed to the fireplace and, reaching behind the spray that had been draped across the mantel, she extracted a charred piece of wood.

"I wondered why that was there," Robert murmured when he joined her. "I nearly tossed it into the fireplace." He aimed a look of feigned shock at the servants, who grinned at seeing his antics.

"Good thing you didn't, or we wouldn't have good luck this year." She gave him the wood.

"Luck?" he repeated, holding up the charred wood. "This little piece of charcoal is supposed to bring luck?"

Ivy gave a shrug. "It's for continuity," she explained. "We use a piece of last year's log to light this year's log."

"Very well." Robert turned to address the servants, who were once again lined up in a semi-circle. "I had quite forgotten how many people worked here at Ritchfield Park," he said after clearing his throat. "I won't keep you. I know you're quite busy with preparing food and cleaning and whatnot," he added. He turned to Ivy. "Her ladyship has asked that I do the honors of lighting this log from last year's remnant." He touched the candle's flame to the charred wood until it lit. Carefully lowering it into the fireplace, he tucked it against some kindling at one end of the Yule log, and within seconds, flames erupted from the base of the large log.

The servants cheered and applauded.

"I understand some dancing is to happen?" he said, his attention on Ivy.

She stepped forward and said, "It's not mandatory, of course, but like we have done for other Christmas Eves, we'd like it if you'd join us here in the hall for some music and dancing after your dinner."

"Which is nearly ready, my lady," the cook said.

"Thank you, Clara. Once the food has been delivered to the dining room for his lordship's meal, there's no need to continue to wait on us," Ivy said. "Help yourselves to an early dinner, and we'll assemble here in the hall afterwards. By then it should be comfortably warm in here," she added, rubbing her hands over her arms.

The servants sounded their agreements at hearing the plans for the evening, hurrying off to the kitchen when the countess made shoo'ing motions with her hands.

Robert chuckled as he watched them go, pulling Ivy into his arms once they were alone. "They adore you," he murmured.

"They are happy to be working for *you*," she countered.

"I don't know why. Besides Graves, I don't think I've met any of them before."

Ivy gave him a quelling glance. "A few of them are new since you were last here," she agreed. "But most have been here for a decade or more, and they have come to call Ritchfield Park their home."

He stared down at her a moment, as if he was contemplating kissing her again. Noise from the direction of the kitchen had him releasing his hold on her, and his brows furrowed. "Are we changing for dinner?" he asked, his gaze following the line of servants bringing platters of food and bottles of wine into the dining room.

"We are not," she said.

"Good, because I'm starving. All this work on the greenery… I seem to have developed an appetite."

The look he aimed in her direction suggested he was referring to a different sort of appetite, but Ivy pretended not to notice.

CHAPTER 14
A DINNER LEADS TO MORE

A few minutes later

The sound of murmured conversations amongst the staff faded as they made their way back to the kitchen, and the household grew quiet again.

Ivy threaded her arm through Robert's elbow as they headed towards the dining room. "Thank you again for giving Walker your blessing. Salisbury is over-the-moon happy about the prospect of marrying him," she said. "I mentioned to Walker I would be going to York after the holiday, so I am wondering... do you think they could marry there? Would they be allowed?"

Robert lifted a shoulder. "I'll see to it they can wed anywhere they wish," he murmured, understanding they would be far from their own parishes. He led them into the dining room and inhaled deeply, the scents of roasted meats and vegetables filling the air. "Given what's happened with them, I am glad I came to Ritchfield Park. I'm glad you came," he added.

"Oh, I wouldn't have missed this," she replied. "I come to Ritchfield Park nearly every Christmas."

He chuckled as held her chair for her. Just as she had requested the night before, her place setting had been set up adjacent to his. "Which is no doubt why I had such an odd welcome the day before yesterday." He took his seat at the carver and regarded the number of platters on the table with an arched brow.

"Whatever do you mean?" Ivy asked in alarm. She placed her napkin on her lap and held out a platter of sliced ham in his direction.

He lifted a shoulder. "Graves looked at me as if I'd grown horns and a tail," he complained.

"He did not," she argued, thinking he was teasing her.

"Actually, he did," Robert said, his brow arching again. "I don't believe he knew who I was."

Ivy inhaled sharply before she guffawed. "Were you covered in snow and looking like a ghost?" she asked, helping herself to a slice of ham.

He suddenly chuckled as he helped himself to the roast potatoes and then seemed confused as to what to choose next from the dishes on the table. "Probably. It was snowing rather hard, now that you mention it." He put some sliced carrots on his plate and on hers. "Do you always bring ham and beef and gifts for the servants when you come here?"

She nodded. "I do," she admitted, selecting a roll from a basket.

"I'm sorry I didn't know," he said. "Had I known, I would have brought something besides a purse of coins from York."

Ivy paused in dishing some peas onto his plate. "You brought money for the servants?"

He nodded. "I acquired some for the Gladstone Hall staff and left them for Sanderson to distribute on Christmas Day," he explained. "Brought the rest with me and gave them to Graves to do the same for this household." He regarded her with a curious expression. "I didn't think to do it for the townhouse in London."

"Oh, I took care of it before I left," she assured him. "I always bring oranges for the staff here, and Graves knows to put them into boxes for the servants." She finished dishing up some food and regarded her plate as if she didn't know where to start. "He does a rot job with the ribbons on the boxes, but I want them to be a surprise for the servants."

Robert chuckled softly. "If you do it every year, don't you think they're expecting them? The oranges, I mean?" he chided.

"Maybe they are, but if I change the fruit or the number of pieces, then it's still a surprise," she argued.

Surveying the remaining dishes on the table, Robert scoffed. "There's enough food here for our entire family."

"Cook—she goes by Clara—she always likes to make an impression," she said. "And enough to be sure there are leftovers for the servants to take to their families on Boxing Day."

"She is the one servant I recognized besides Graves and Walker," he remarked.

Ivy took a bite of glazed ham, grinning when she tasted the sweet and salty meat. "Whatever we don't eat, the servants will be able to take to their families in Castleford," she reminded him. "Should they be able to make it there the day after Christmas, given all this snow."

"Hopefully the weather will clear by then," Robert said, pouring wine for them both.

They ate their dinner in relative silence, the two occasionally glancing at one another as if they expected the other one to speak.

"The ham is excellent," Robert finally remarked.

"As are the roasted potatoes," Ivy said.

"What's under that cover?" he asked, indicating the platter farthest from them.

"That will be the dessert," she said, reaching over to lift the lid to reveal slices of fruitcake covered with sugared frosting.

He inhaled sharply, sniffing the air. "How much rum do you suppose Clara put into those cakes?" he asked in alarm.

Ivy tittered. "Probably the entire bottle I brought from Berry Brothers. Less whatever she imbibed whilst *making* the cakes," she added in a teasing grin.

Robert guffawed. "Are the servants having it for dessert as well?"

She nodded. "Probably."

He continued to laugh. "Perhaps I shall have to serve them some port after dinner," he said. "Besides the coins, it's all I brought with me from York."

Ivy blinked. "Are you thinking to *shorten* this evening's festivities?" she asked in alarm.

"Maybe," he admitted.

She giggled. "Robert," she scolded. A moment passed before she said, "I don't know why I was so nervous when I saw you yesterday."

He glanced up from his plate, obviously surprised at the comment. "Well, you weren't exactly expecting me to be here."

"True," she acknowledged. "But... I worried you had finally decided to..." She clamped her mouth shut and closed her eyes.

"Decided to do what?" he prompted.

She audibly sighed. "Divorce me."

His fork clattering onto his plate, Robert stared at his wife with a combination of hurt and shock. "Divorce you?" he repeated in a whisper. "*Never*, Ivy. How could you even think that?"

She opened her eyes and stared at him for several seconds before lifting a shoulder. "Surely you were wishing to get on with your life."

He growled before leaning back in his chair. "I can't imagine doing it with anyone else," he murmured. "Especially after rereading all your letters."

Ivy swallowed. "Before you read them—"

"I never considered there would ever be anyone else," he claimed.

She shook her head when she realized he had misunderstood her meaning. "Before you read those letters, did you... did you ever think of me? During the course of your days—?"

"I do every day. Every night," he said in a low voice. "I wonder whose parlor you are having tea in, and who you are dancing with at the balls, and in whose box you are sitting in at the theatre," he said, his gaze darting to the side. He struggled to keep from adding, *Whose bed you are warming.*

"Oh," she breathed. "Well, I take tea with several different ladies depending on the day of the week," she said, about to list all their names. Seeing his expression change to a grimace, she decided not to mention any names. "You know them all, mavens of gossip and the judges of who shall and who shall not wed in the coming Season," she added with a wave. "I rarely attend the theatre, nor do I dance much these days," she went on. "I would rather watch the younger couples. Sort who I think will make good matches and who would be miserable." She swallowed, deciding to admit her thoughts about him. "You are frequently on my mind as well."

"I am?" He straightened, obviously surprised by the comment.

She nodded. "Of course, Robert. I wonder if you are spending your days in your study or at your club, or if you are on a hunt in the country. Who you are dancing with at the district ball. Whose box you are in at the theatre." She thought better of adding, *Whose bed you are warming.*

He chuckled softly. "Most of my days are spent in my study," he murmured. "I've become quite involved in the coal mining business, especially this past year, what with this awful weather and all," he explained.

"You go to the mines?" she asked in surprise.

"I go to the offices in Wakefield every few weeks," he clarified. "I have a townhouse there. Small staff." He drank some wine. "The men's club in York is more tradesmen and bankers than aristocrats, of course, but given the mines, I suppose I fit in there." He paused a moment. "I haven't been on a hunt in an age. I'm usually in the card room at the balls. I never dance. And I don't attend the theatre unless I must to appease someone, but I think you could have guessed that." He exhaled a breath and shrugged. "Not a very exciting life, I admit."

Ivy sighed again. "I miss you, Robert."

He stared at her for a long moment. "I miss you as well."

Ivy wasn't sure if she stood first or if he did, but the chairs were nearly overturned in their haste to embrace one another. Once they were in each other's arms, his lips took hers with an urgency Ivy hadn't experienced before, the firm pillows suckling hers as his arms tightened their hold around her waist and shoulder.

He kissed her as if his life depended on it.

Perhaps it did.

She returned the kiss in equal measure, sounding a faint moan of relief as if she had been starving for such intimacy.

Perhaps she had.

When his tongue delved into her mouth, sliding over her teeth and tangling with hers, a low groan vibrated in his chest. Ivy could feel it through her day gown and into her bosom, into her middle and down to her toes. She lifted a hand to the side of his head, her fingertips threading through his short hair as her nails scraped his scalp.

The groan turned into a low growl, which only encouraged her to use her other hand to do the same on the other side of his head. She delighted in the feel of his hair, the dark silky strands near his temples mixed with coarser grays, the shorter hairs at his neck softer.

Moving a hand to the side of his face, Ivy realized he might have shaved that morning, but the signs of his dark beard were evident on his otherwise smooth cheeks. The scent of his citrusy cologne wafted across her nostrils.

A moment later his tongue retreated and he softened the kiss. Ivy purred and relaxed into his hold. She had always preferred the less frantic kisses and the way his hand smoothed up and down her back, its warmth permeating the muslin of her day gown. She couldn't help but inhale sharply when his wandering hand moved to her side and his thumb brushed the side of her breast, briefly interrupting the kiss.

He managed to recapture her lips, though, breaking off the soft chuckle that she could feel more than hear. In response, she slid a hand to just below one of his ears and captured his earlobe between her thumb and the the side of her forefinger. She gently tugged on it before smoothing her thumb along the tender skin.

This time, it was he who had to break off the kiss to inhale sharply, his whispered, "Minx," sounding loud in her ears.

He continued to kiss her as if he was making up for all the years they hadn't done this.

Perhaps he was.

At some point, either Perkins or Graves had come to the dining room to collect their plates, but neither Robert nor Ivy acknowledged the gasp of embarrassment or the murmured, "Pardon me," as the servant scurried back to the butler's pantry.

When he finally released her lips, their shared expressions of surprise and embarrassment turned into tentative grins. Robert allowed a long sigh. "I could not help it," he said, as if he was apologizing for having kissed her. "After what happened on the Yule log, I wanted to kiss you again. Wanted to kiss you the moment I found you in my bed last night," he admitted.

Ivy purred. "Is that all?" She grinned. "At least you knew it was me and not a dream," she added in a tease.

His silver-blue eyes seemed to darken in response. "You know it is not," he whispered.

Ivy's face, already flushed with color, seemed to redden even more. "Well, you'll have me, I promise. But not until after the dancing is done," she replied, her own eyes darkening as if in warning.

"So... I can't have you right now? For dessert?" he asked meekly, glancing at the table. "Right here?"

Ivy blinked. "Robert," she scolded. She glanced towards the butler's pantry and then to the door. Although she didn't exactly have a plan, she thought to move to the end of the table and lift her skirts when Graves suddenly appeared at the door.

"Pardon me, my lord. My lady," he said, obviously surprised to find them standing. "The servants have finished their meal, the refreshment table has been set, and the pianoforté has been uncovered."

Robert made a sound of frustration. "We haven't eaten any of the fruitcake," he complained, although from the way he said it, Ivy knew he meant something entirely different.

"We'll be there in a moment, Graves," she said. "But could you bring the fruitcake and set it at the refreshment table? I'd like to share it with everyone."

"Of course, my lady," Graves answered nervously, moving to do her bidding.

Ivy tugged on Robert's hand. "Come, darling," she whispered.

"My coat is in my study," he said, leading them there first. "Am I going to have to give a speech again?"

She paused on the threshold. "Well, you could remind them they don't have to work on Boxing Day," she suggested. "And that they should keep their champagne consumption to no more than two glasses." She helped him with his top coat and buttoned it.

Robert scoffed. "Champagne?" he repeated in surprise. "You... you brought champagne? For the servants?"

Ivy nodded. "A few bottles. You brought port," she accused. When he rolled his eyes, she tittered. "Oh, it's nearly Christmas, Robert," she reminded him. "And tonight, we are celebrating."

He seemed to pout for a moment before he asked, "Will I get an orange?"

Ivy grinned as they made their way into the decorated hall. "I'll see to it you have two," she replied happily.

CHAPTER 15
DANCING AND MERRIMENT

minute later

Several servants had already gathered in the great hall when Ivy and Robert joined them. Some were dressed in their Sunday best and similarly coiffed for the Christmas Eve event while others were still dressed as they had been to make the decorations. Those who had been in service to the Ritchfield earldom for more than a year or two knew what to expect on this night—an enjoyable evening of dancing and merriment, of games and gifts.

The trestle had been pushed to the side of the great hall and was dressed in a red linen tablecloth. Glasses were lined up on it, and several bottles of champagne were set in buckets filled with snow.

The kissing bough, featuring apples, flowers and small dolls, had been hung just inside the front door. Although no one was expected to come through the door given the awful weather, Ivy knew that particular location would become more popular as the evening progressed.

Barbara, already dressed for the evening's entertainments,

appeared from the kitchens. Her arms were laden with a large salver of sugared plums and fruit cake.

When he saw the scullery maid, Robert leaned over and whispered, "I should have dressed more formally." He nodded to the servants when they curtsied and bowed.

"Nonsense. This is not a formal occasion," Ivy countered. "You can dress for the Twelfth Night celebration if you'd like."

Robert displayed a frown. "What? We're doing this all again in a fortnight?" he complained.

Ivy patted his arm. "You're the master of the house, so if you don't wish to—"

"They'll expect it, won't they?" he interrupted.

"Probably," she agreed, turning her smile on her lady's maid. Anne and Tom were standing next to one another, her arm threaded through his elbow, as were Bobby and Christina. Bobby held his violin and bow, obviously waiting for a cue from the earl to begin the music. "I'm going to start playing the piano-forté, but if you should like to dance with me, Mrs. Ashton can perform in my place," Ivy said, nodding in Christina's direction.

Robert tugged on her hand, "I haven't danced in an age," he reminded her.

"Neither have I."

Ivy made her way to the piano-forté, and Bobby joined her. When she had the sheet music in place, the two began to play.

Maids lined up on one side of the hall while the men did so on the other, and given there were more women, Robert gingerly joined the line of men for the longways dance that ensued. A Scottish reel followed, which had the servants quickly forming into two circles of four, and laughter ensued when Perkins couldn't quite keep up.

Breathless at the end, Robert stepped away from the others and moved to the refreshment table. He nearly downed his champagne in a single gulp, and soon, others joined him. He took the opportunity to address the servants again.

"I don't wish to take too much of your time on this evening, but I do have a couple of announcements. First," he waved for Tom and Anne to step forward. "I have the honor of sharing the news that the Mr. Walker has proposed marriage and Miss Salisbury has accepted."

Although the news didn't seem to come as a surprise to most, applause and cheers erupted from the servants. When they quieted, Robert said, "Two days from now—Boxing Day —will be a day for you to do as you wish. You of course will not be expected to work at all for the entire day or night."

A murmur of appreciation sounded.

"With any luck—we should certainly have some given we've all taken a seat on the Yule log—the weather will cooperate, and you'll be able to go to visit your families, or go shopping in Castleford, or spend the day in quiet contemplation," he continued. "My countess has seen to it you'll all be receiving an orange or two this evening."

"Maybe three," Ivy said from where she sat in front of the piano-forté, lining up the next sheet music.

Her comment was met with chuckles.

"As for tomorrow, I rather doubt it will be possible to go to church, so please know you are welcome to use the chapel here at Ritchfield Park." He turned and arched a brow in Ivy's direction. When she responded with a nod, he said. "Please feel free to stay up and dance as long as you'd like, even after her ladyship and I have retired." He paused. "And with that, let the dancing resume."

Ivy and Bobby played "L'Hipparchia", a piece appropriate for a quadrille. One of the maids called out for a waltz, and when they were about to begin the appropriate three-count music, Robert gave Christina a beseeching glance. "Do you mind playing this one?" he asked.

"I would be honored, my lord," she said, hurrying over to the piano-forté.

Robert motioned for Bobby to continue playing, and he took Ivy's hand from the keyboard to kiss the back of it. "Will you do me the honor of dancing with me?" he asked.

"I thought you would never ask," she said, sliding off the bench. Christina quickly took her place, and although her playing skills weren't as refined as Ivy's, she managed to keep tempo with her husband's playing.

The earl and countess joined the circle of other dancers already engaged in the waltz, the hems of gowns swinging in arcs as the couples moved about the hall.

"I do hope you're enjoying yourself," Ivy said, her face flushed from the dance.

Robert turned her under his arm and recaptured her hand in his. "I am, but I think it's time we left the servants to their merriment," he said. "What about you?"

"I haven't given them their gifts yet," she said in protest.

Robert nodded in the direction of the refreshments table, where Graves was lining up pasteboard boxes adorned with ribbons. "You can do so when we finish this dance," he said.

"Where did *those* boxes come from?" she asked in surprise. "They are far nicer than the ones we usually use," she added in awe.

He chuckled softly. "I might have found them earlier. In one of the trunks Perkins brought down from the attic," he hinted. "They were flattened, but Graves assured me he could make them presentable, and it appears he has."

"I think he must have had one of the maids make the bows," Ivy remarked. "They look positively beautiful."

"Indeed. I hope you don't mind, but I had him put the coins in the boxes with the oranges."

Ivy's eyes rounded. "Robert," she said on a breath.

"It's only a few coins, but... I thought it only right since I'm having the butler at Gladstone Hall do the same thing."

"With oranges, too?" she asked in surprise.

He grimaced. "Apples, actually. Oh, and enough money in Mr. Walker's box so he can buy a marriage license," he added. "He won't be able to get one at his own parish in London."

She tittered as the music ended, leaving them next to the front door.

Robert glanced up and Ivy followed his gaze. "Oh," she whispered, discovering the kissing bough hung directly above their heads.

"Oh, indeed," he said, before capturing her lips with his. Although the kiss was short, it was a prelude of what he intended to be doing once they were in his bedchamber.

The two quietly made their way up the stairs, sure they wouldn't be missed.

CHAPTER 16
GIFTS TO MAKE MERRY

few minutes later
"Have they already gone upstairs?" Tom asked, his eyes sweeping the hall when the next dance had ended.

Anne gave him a look of disbelief. "You didn't notice them take their leave?"

Tom shook his head and regarded her with a grin. "I think because I only have had eyes for you on this night."

Her face coloring even more with his comment—the dancing had been the other reason she displayed a blush—Anne leaned in closer and said, "Her ladyship told me she wouldn't require my services 'til morning."

His eyes darkened, but then Graves cleared his throat and the two, along with everyone else, were forced to turn their attention to the head servant.

"His lordship has seen to it you each have a gift for Christmas, so before you retire this evening, you'll want to look for a box with your name on it," he said, waving a hand at the refreshments table. "I am also to remind you there is more champagne, although might I suggest you drink no more than two glasses? We do have some work to do on the morrow. That is all."

A round of chuckles erupted before the servants rushed to the table.

The boxes, each wrapped with a ribbon and topped with a red bow, had tags on them with their names written in ink. At the sound of jingling when they were jostled, several gasps could be heard.

"There is money in mine," one of the housemaids said with excitement, after she had torn off the ribbon and peeked inside.

"Mine as well," Christina said.

"Mine, too," Perkins chimed in, although he was holding one of the oranges he found in his box against his chest as if it was the real gold.

"Everyone received the same amount of blunt," Graves stated, "Along with three oranges."

"Her ladyship is so generous," Bobby remarked. "She is the one who brought the oranges from London. I know because I hauled 'em in from her coach yesterday."

"As is his lordship," Graves countered soberly. "The blunt is from him."

"I hope we can go to Castleford on Boxing Day," Anne said. "I would so like to go shopping."

Tom was staring into his box, stunned to discover that besides the coins and oranges, his contained several bank notes along with a short note. He plucked the parchment from the box and unfolded it.

For the marriage license. Best wishes. Ritchfield.

"What is it?" Anne asked, stepping closer when she noticed he was reading. "Is it good news?"

"The very best," Tom said, allowing a broad grin. He lowered his voice and added, "Do not fret, my love, for I will get us to Castleford."

She grinned and watched as some of the other servants bid everyone good-night and headed towards the servants' stairs at the back of the house. Instead of following, she helped Barbara and Clara take the leftover cakes and glasses to the kitchen.

"It was good of your husband to bring you tonight," Anne said, nodding to Mr. Godfrey. He had joined the merriment at some point that evening, when it was apparent more men were needed for the dancing. "The trip through the snow must have been quite a challenge."

"It wasn't bad between here and the farm," Mr. Godfrey said. "And it's not as cold now as it was yesterday, so we're going to head home straight away."

"Safe travels," Tom said, joining them in the kitchen. "Bobby and I saw to the horses before dinner. Is there anything else that's needin' to be done before I retire?"

Clara made a shoo'ing motion with her hands. "Off wif' all of you," she said. "I need my beauty sleep if I'm goin' to be up at dawn to make the bread for breakfast."

"Well, then happy Christmas," Anne said.

"Happy Christmas," several replied in unison, some making their way upstairs while others saw to restoring the hall to the way it was before the dancing had begun.

Tom and Anne were the last of the servants to climb the stairs, and he gripped her hand and pulled her onto the first floor. "I'd understand if you'd rather not make love with me again so soon, but I would like to at least hold you whilst you sleep," he whispered.

Anne's eyes rounded. "Why wouldn't I?" she asked in alarm.

He opened his mouth to respond and seemed to think better of it. "Oh, I am going to have a very happy Christmas then, aren't I?" he said before they hurried off down the corridor, their Christmas boxes jingling in the dark.

"Did you ever doubt it?" Anne countered.

CHAPTER 17
A CHRISTMAS EVE OF RECONCILIATION

*E*arlier, on the main stairs

Once he and Ivy were up a flight of stairs and out of earshot of the servants, Robert took Ivy's hand in his. "You will come with me to my bedchamber?" he asked.

The query made it sound as if he feared she would deny him, but Ivy had no intention of turning him down. With her skirts gathered into her free hand, she was practically racing him up the stairs. "Of course, I will. Will you undo my buttons?" she countered, before she burst through the master bedchamber door.

"I've a mind to simply tear your gown off of you," Robert countered, following her into the room as if he were being chased. Before she could put voice to a protest, he added, "But I won't since I rather like seeing you in it."

Ivy reached for his top coat and quickly undid the buttons. "That's a relief. I shouldn't want my new lady's maid to have to do a repair so soon." She pushed the coat from his shoulders and went to work on his waistcoat buttons.

"Even if I tore it off you, there are no doubt layers of underthings I still have to remove," he complained, attempting to undo the buttons at her back while she was facing him.

"What underthings?"

His eyes widened as his fingers stilled. "The sorts you wear under your gowns?" he ventured.

A slight look of disappointment appeared at the corner of her lips. "Oh, for a moment, I was thinking of what I wore last night," she whispered. "Or rather, didn't. I suppose there are some stays and petticoats that must come off from under this one," she added on a sigh.

Robert blinked before his gaze fell to her bosom. The telltale signs of hardened nipples were evident in the muslin. "Do you mean to tell me you were naked under your gown throughout our entire dinner last night?" he asked in amazement, his breathing still coming in pants from their quick trip up the stairs. He let go of a fastening at her back when she forced the waistcoat from his torso.

"Of course. Petticoats ruin the line of a satin gown, and my regular stays tend to show at the edges of the neckline," she explained, reaching down to undo the closures on his breeches. "So I had to wear the smaller stays."

He placed a hand over hers. "Had I known that, *you* would have been last night's dessert," he stated.

"Robert," she murmured, pulling her hands from beneath his to resume her work.

"I need to remove my shoes first, my sweet," he said in a whisper. He backed up to the bed and shed the footwear before seeing to his stockings.

Meanwhile, Ivy rushed to the bed to turn down the counterpane and linens, her actions creating a wind and sending the flames in the fireplace into a frenzy. Embers danced about on the hearth.

"Careful, or you'll start another fire," he teased, pushing the breeches from his legs.

She stepped in front of him and went to work on untying his cravat. "I suppose I should remind you it's been years since you've seen me... unclothed," she whispered. "The last few times we did this, it was dark. I expect you'll be a bit disappointed."

"I rather doubt that," he said, helping her to unwind the length of silk from around his neck. As she lifted up the hem of his shirt, he was attempting to push the sleeves of her gown down her arms. When neither could continue what they were trying to do, they stopped and chuckled softly.

"You first," he said, giving up his hold on her gown to raise his arms over his head.

Ivy had the shirt removed from his torso a moment later, and when her gown was free of her arms, it slid down her body into a puddle of fabric on the carpet below. The petticoats, stays, and chemise soon followed.

When she caught him staring at her mostly naked body— she still wore a pair of stockings—she lifted her arms in front of her chest in an attempt to hide her breasts from his view.

He was too quick.

"Oh, no you don't," he said, gathering her into his arms so she was pressed hard against the front of his body.

"Oh," she managed, before his lips took hers in a scorching kiss. Wrapping her arms around his neck, she stood on tiptoes and was rewarded when one of his hands skimmed down the side of her body and over one of the globes of her bottom.

"Your hand is so warm," she whispered once he had ended the kiss to take a much-needed breath.

"That's not the only thing that's warm," he murmured.

Ivy was well aware of his manhood, its hardened length pressed into her soft belly. "I do believe you're the one who is in danger of starting another fire," she accused.

He chuckled softly before lifting her into his arms. "God,

but I've missed you," he said, before dumping her onto the bed.

She gasped when her bare back hit the cold linens and gasped again when he crawled atop her. "I've missed you," she whispered, spreading her legs in anticipation of him impaling her. Instead, he was kissing his way down the front of her body. "Where are you going?" she asked, giving up her hold on his shoulders.

He chuckled and mumbled something incoherent, and a moment later, Ivy inhaled sharply when his whiskers scraped the insides of her thighs. "Robert!"

The sensation of his thumbs and tongue on her most private place had her attempting to pull her knees together. She stopped when the first frissons skittered through her thighs and belly. "Oh!" When his tongue circled her womanhood, she mewled first in protest and then in pleasure until whatever he was doing had her insides tumbling about in a maelstrom of welcome sensations. When the frissons coalesced into a single wave of pleasure, she cried out, her hands reaching down to cup the sides of his head. "You have to stop," she whimpered, her breaths sounding labored.

She felt more than heard his chuckle and inhaled sharply when he was once again atop her. She inhaled again at the sensation of the tip of his manhood at her entrance. "Hurry," she whispered.

"We have all night," he countered, although his entry into her was quick. Both of them gasped when he was suddenly buried to the hilt. "Oh, Ivy," he breathed. He pulled nearly all the way out of her before thrusting into her again.

Her hips met his on his next thrust, and he groaned. "I was going to make this last," he murmured, as if in protest.

"Next time," she managed between gasps for breath.

He growled in response, and from the way his body seized and his face lifted, she knew he was in the throes of his orgasm. Deep within, she felt his last desperate thrust as the wash of warmth filled her, and she sighed happily.

*B*reathing heavily, Robert rolled off of Ivy and landed on his back, groaning as he did so.

Tittering, Ivy turned her head and regarded him with a grin. "How is it we can be so good together when we're in a bed and so... distant with one another when we're out of one?"

He regarded her with an expression of hurt. "I don't think that's an entirely fair assessment of us at all," he replied, sliding his arm beneath her shoulders in an effort to pull her closer. "Our first few years of marriage were rather pleasant, as I recall." He grunted. "Our first twenty years, even."

"That's because we spent most of them in bed," she countered, grinning with the memory.

Robert rubbed a hand over his face, felt the evening stubble of his beard. "How could we not? When you were expecting Charity, you were insatiable," he accused. "You were the same with Grace and Michael, too."

She giggled softly. "You were so accommodating."

"I had to be your cock on demand," he said on an exaggerated sigh. "I was afraid you might decide a footman was good enough."

Gasping, Ivy turned her head to regard him with disbelief. "Never," she responded. "Eww."

He guffawed. "I'll never forget the time you sent a footman to Parliament with a note saying my presence was required post-haste. I don't think I ever had Walker drive the town coach as fast as he did that day. I was sure I was going to arrive to find the house on fire, and instead, I discovered you, bare naked, round with child..." He motioned the shape of a ball with a hand over his own midsection. "In the middle of my bed, demanding my cock."

She grinned at the reminder of what had occurred when she was pregnant with their first son, Michael. "I was so in need of you," she insisted. "Right up until the end. And as I recall, you didn't seem to mind one bit."

Once again sounding a guffaw, he said, "That's because I was able to leave an especially boring session of Parliament. Some ancient earl was droning on about corn or wheat or some such." He turned to look at her. "You were far more fun to plow."

She reached out and slapped a hand on his thigh. "Don't be crass," she scolded.

They both sighed, and Robert reached for her hand with one of his. He brought it to his lips and kissed the palm. "I spent so many nights wondering..."

She stared at him, her auburn brows crinkling. "Wondering what?"

He displayed a grimace. "More of a whom," he murmured. "I was sure you had taken a lover in London. I feared I even knew his identity—"

"*What?*" she interrupted, pulling back her hand so she could lift herself up on her elbows. As a result, the bed linens shifted so her breasts were exposed. She stared down at him. "I don't have a lover," she claimed. "That's what you thought? All this time?"

Robert swallowed, his gaze going briefly to her nipples. He rolled onto his side, pressed an elbow into the mattress, and held his head on his hand. "Did you ever think about taking one?" he asked, before leaning forward to kiss the side of the breast closest to him. He closed his eyes and buried his nose in the soft flesh, his eyelids barely touching her skin.

She inhaled sharply at the tickling sensation. "No. Never,"

she insisted, lowering herself back onto the bed and pulling up the linens so she was once again covered.

Emitting a sound of disappointment, Robert furrowed a brow even as he felt profound relief at hearing her declaration. "All these years... and you haven't made love to anyone?"

She blinked and swallowed. "Robert, you have a terrible memory," she accused.

"What are you saying?"

"Every Season when you're in London..." She paused, her eyes narrowing. "Don't tell me you actually slept through all those times I sneaked into your bedchamber when I was in need of you."

Robert furrowed his brows. "That was *you*?" he asked in a whisper.

She made a sound of disgust and once again sat up. "Well, who else would it be?"

He shook his head. "That *was* you," he said again. "I always thought I was... I was *dreaming*," he said softly. "Now you're telling me you were... it *was* you who was seducing me in the middle of the night?"

She scoffed in disbelief. "You thought it was someone else?"

He shrugged. "I didn't know. It was dark, and I thought I was dreaming," he murmured. "You were quite the seductress," he accused, a grin lifting the corner of his mouth.

"I didn't exactly have to *seduce* you," she claimed with a huff. She crossed her arms over her chest. "You were always quite welcoming as I recall."

"Oh, no doubt," he murmured.

"Hard as a rock."

"In my sleep?"

She lifted a shoulder. "Well, I didn't know you were *sleeping* through it," she countered defensively.

"Was... was I atop you?" There was only a hint of a tease in his voice, but Ivy caught it. She let out another sound of disbelief and stared at him before saying, "Sometimes, and sometimes I was." She waggled her eyebrows.

"Riding St. George," he whispered. "I always loved it when you did that. Your gorgeous breasts bouncing up and down. Your hair all loose and long, the ends of it brushing over my chest." He sighed as he settled back onto the mattress.

She angled her head to one side. "So you *do* remember?"

Robert inhaled and shook his head. "I wish I'd been wide awake instead of half asleep. No wonder there were days when I woke up so happy," he said, arching his brow. "The bed linens were all mussed as if I'd been fighting off the ghosts."

Inhaling sharply, Ivy stared at him. "What did you say?"

He cleared his throat and reached out an arm in an attempt to bring her closer to him. When she finally relaxed and snuggled against his side, her head in the small of his shoulder, he said, "Nothing."

She lifted her head to stare at him. "Were those the same ghosts you spoke of with Graves?" she asked. "What we talked about earlier?"

He narrowed his eyes. "Did... did he tell you that?"

"I heard it from my new lady's maid," she said. "I might have... *encouraged* her to share what she had heard about your unexpected arrival. 'The ghosts of the past have driven me from York'," she added. "Are there other ghosts, Robert?" she asked. "Ones you haven't told me about?"

He inhaled deeply and let the breath out in a *whoosh*. "Aren't they enough?" he asked on a sigh. "I admit, I have been feeling my age these days. Spending too much time wondering if I've done right by you. By our children. By my title—"

"Of course you have," she insisted. "Robert," she added in a gentle scold.

"Those first few years after I inherited were so hard," he murmured.

Ivy lifted her head. "Because?" she prompted.

He winced. "Father's debts. I felt as if we were mired in a giant gaping morass."

Although Ivy hadn't been with him back then—she hadn't even had her come-out when he inherited—she knew a bit about his early struggles with the earldom. He'd had to sell off a number of unentailed properties to come up with enough blunt to pay off creditors and the vowels left behind. Although he was essentially debt-free at the time of their marriage, there were still a few years when he ran the earldom as if he was still in debt. "And yet you paid them all off," she said brightly.

"I didn't think it fair you had to economize as a result, though," he murmured. "Those first few years."

She shrugged. "I didn't mind. As I recall, I didn't know I was economizing," she said. "It wasn't as if it was going to be like that forever."

"I don't think I ever told you how much I appreciated your efforts to help when it came to your wardrobe and to buying things for the children and the house."

"I didn't mind wearing the same gowns two years in a row," she said. "But I do wish you had told me before we returned from our wedding trip. So I wouldn't have had the salon and dining room redone at Gladstone. The cost of the tassels for the drapes and sofa alone was enough to put us back into debt," she claimed, remembering how stunned she had been when she peeked at the invoice. "The renovations could have waited."

A grunt sounded from him. "I didn't want to take that from you. It made you happy to have such a project, and it did improve Gladstone greatly, even if I didn't actually notice the improvements at first."

She gave him a quelling glance. "I gave you an entire week to say something before I scolded you," she reminded him.

"I noticed the changes in the dining room right away," he countered.

"I should hope so. The walls were covered in a completely different colored fabric, and I had the colorman redo the paint for the mouldings. You would have had to be blind not to notice."

"The Turkish rug in there is still my favorite," he murmured.

She grinned and hummed contentedly. "You haven't had it changed?"

He chuckled. "Nothing has changed since your last visit," he replied. "Except for a few servants."

"As I recall, it didn't take long for you to pay off your father's accounts."

He shook his head in the pillow. "Cold winters helped. The coal mines... well, they were more profitable than I expected," he admitted.

"Probably because you didn't trust them to an unscrupulous man of business as your father did," she reasoned. "Nor have you ever been much of a gambler. At least, if you were, you never mentioned it."

"True. Besides, owning mines is enough of a gamble." He ran a hand down the side of her arm until he could grip her hand in his. "But it did mean I had to spend an awful lot of time on the business. Away from you and the children."

"You were never gone longer than a fortnight, and you always came back. The children still recognized you, so it wasn't as if you were gone too long," she teased.

He chuckled. "I suppose that was something, although there were times I didn't recognize the children."

"You did better than some of your fellow peers," she whispered.

"How so?"

She tittered. "I heard Lord Pettigrew didn't even meet his heir until the boy returned from Eton."

Robert let out a guffaw. "I was a bit more involved with my children than most," he agreed. "I didn't want them growing up to be cold-hearted bastards like so many of my fellow peers. Like my father. Forgive the curse."

She sighed. "You're forgiven."

"Truth be told, I didn't want to be away from you at all," he murmured. "I feared I would come home to discover you had some young buck... bucking you," he stammered. "Don't think I didn't overhear my peers remarking on your generous bosom or your gorgeous hair and how much they wanted a chance to plow you."

"Robert Michael John Lucius Strathford—"

"Ah. I'm in trouble now," he said, rolling his eyes before he scoffed softly. "You remembered all my names," he added, as if he was impressed.

"Of course I remember all your names," she replied. "How else am I to ensure you know when I'm annoyed with you?"

He displayed another grimace. "As I recall, you didn't used to say anything. For sometimes an entire day," he murmured.

She inhaled to respond but bit her lip. It was another moment before she said, "That's because I feared I would say too much, and you would leave, go to your mistress, and never come back."

Robert suddenly sat up in the bed, which once again had the bed linens coming off of her. He turned to stare at her in disbelief. "What mistress?"

Blinking, Ivy gripped the bed linens tighter to her chest. "Whichever one you happened to employ at the time, I suppose," she said meekly.

He growled and rolled his eyes again. "Ivy Anne Charity Strathford, I most certainly did not employ a mistress," he claimed. "At least, not after we were married. How... how could you think such a thing?"

Ivy inhaled at his mention of all her names. "Well, a... a prostitute then," she countered in a hoarse whisper, not about to give up her argument.

"Eww," he responded, his face displaying disgust. "Never. Besides, why the... why the *fuck* would I want to bed another woman when I had you as a wife?"

She recoiled at the vehemence in his query. "Well, why indeed?" she countered, sitting up to challenge him. Having used her hands to help in the process, the bed linens fell from her chest and once again left her front on display.

His gaze dropped to her breasts, the orbs still rather pert despite her age. "Why ever would I want any other woman?" he asked in a whisper.

Ivy inhaled softly. "Did you... did you want me because of my bosom? Or... or because of my hair?"

Blinking, he allowed a soft chuckle. "Neither."

"What?" she asked in disbelief.

He grinned at seeing her expression. "The first time I saw you—"

"Was where?" she challenged.

"At your presentation before the queen," he said without a pause. "All the other debutantes your age came out looking like they were being led to the lions, but not you," he said on a soft chuckle. "You came out with a smile on your face, as if you thought it was the best day of your life, your gorgeous eyes lit up like green fire."

Ivy gasped at hearing his recollection. "You noticed... my *eyes*?" she asked in wonder.

His expression suggested he was still recalling that day, thirty years ago. "Yes," he affirmed. He suddenly sobered and turned to stare at her. "What did you think I noticed?"

She gave him a quelling glance and straightened so the bed linens once again exposed her bosom.

He raised his brows in appreciation. "I do adore them. And your hair. More than you can know," he admitted.

They sat together on the bed in companionable silence for a time before Ivy said, "I can't believe you thought I took a lover."

His expression turning sheepish, Robert winced. "I'm terribly jealous," he admitted, leaning over to kiss her on the corner of her mouth. "It's hard not to think the worst when you have the most beautiful woman as a wife—"

She scoffed softly.

"—and you're not a particularly handsome bloke."

Her mouth dropping open in surprise, Ivy stared at him a moment. "You don't think you're handsome?" she asked softly.

"You don't," he accused with a shrug.

About to counter his claim, she instead dipped her head. "Looks are not all that important in a husband," she murmured. When he grunted in response, she added, "Besides, you never had to be." She moved a finger to where the dark whorls at the base of his torso disappeared beneath the edge of the bed linens.

He inhaled sharply at her touch, his manhood already hardening in readiness. "What are you saying?"

"I remember seeing you that day. The day of my presentation to the queen," she said, lifting her chin. "From the first moment I saw you, I wanted you, and I didn't know why," she admitted.

He grunted. "As I recall, I was standing with a half-dozen other peers, several younger and far more handsome than me," he said, doubting her claim.

"It was your eyes, Robert."

Giving a start, Robert narrowed them. "My eyes?"

"They're terribly wicked," she said in a whisper. "Sometimes they're silver and sometimes they're blue-gray," she said. "Rather startling, if you've never seen them before. You were staring at me that day, like you could see *through* me," she whispered, her body shivering. "Or mayhap just through my gown. It was... unsettling, but exciting, too, the way my body reacted. I think I experienced my first orgasm at that moment." She took a breath and let it out. "Just part of your charisma I suppose."

He stared at her for several seconds, as if he was seeing her in an entirely different light. "I wasn't aware," he whispered.

She lifted her gaze to meet his as her hand wrapped around his manhood and squeezed. "I... I didn't understand attraction. Desire. Lust."

He feathered his lips over her forehead. "I remember later that night," he whispered softly. "At the queen's ball. I was all set to ravish you in the gardens—"

"And I was going to let you, even though I had no idea what that meant."

"—kiss you senseless—"

"Oh, you're very good at that. You always have been."

"—claim your maidenhead for myself—"

"I'm rather glad our first time was in a bed."

"—and do it all over again and again and again."

Mewling softly, Ivy allowed her head to drop back on her shoulders as his kisses tickled her neck. She was forced to let go of his member when he pushed her down to the bed so he could take one of her breasts with his mouth.

"I remember the first time you did this, you said more than a mouthful was a waste when it came to breasts," she whispered.

Robert lifted his mouth from her skin to murmur, "I was a fool. A stupid fool." He recaptured her nipple and nibbled it before moving his attentions to her other breast. "I am so much wiser now."

She giggled and raised her knees in invitation. "Ah, yes, but right now I need the foolish you," she begged.

He chuckled and did her bidding, burying his manhood into her wet and willing channel. Before he began the movements that would send them both to the edge of oblivion, he kissed her softly. "Ivy Anne Charity, I don't know what sort of spell you've cast over me," he growled as she lifted her knees to grip his thighs. "I think I am falling in love with you all over again."

"Well, it's about damned time," she whispered with a grin. "We've been married nearly thirty—" She inhaled sharply when he did something with a strategically placed thumb.

"Still works," he whispered, feathering his fingertips over her mound.

She visibly shivered beneath him, and for the first time in a decade, he once again felt true happiness.

Ecstasy was to follow a few minutes later.

CHAPTER 18
A MORNING BATH

The following morning, Christmas Day

As the sounds of the household waking up reached her ears, Ivy stirred but didn't open her eyes. She listened intently to the distant footfalls of servants above and below, to the house as it seemed to groan under its own weight, and to the sound and sensation of her husband's snores.

At some point during the night, he had rested his head against the side of her breast, his nose pressed into the soft flesh. She had a thought he might suffocate if he stayed there too long.

When he took a deep breath and rolled away from her, she felt cool air where his body had been and mourned the loss. She rolled until she was pressed to his back and draped an arm over his middle. A moment later, she felt a kiss on the back of her knuckles.

"I think we've scandalized the servants," she whispered.

Blinking against the sunshine that suddenly streamed into the master bedchamber, Robert held up a hand to shade his face. "Why ever would you say that?" he asked, his voice cracking. He cleared his throat.

"Salisbury just sounded the alarm that I'm not in the mistress suite." She yawned and stretched, humming when she sensed the delicious soreness from having made love more than once the night before.

Robert started to sit up, and then paused when he realized they weren't alone. He was about to put voice to a curse, but managed to stifle the urge.

"Good day, my lord. Do you require a valet this morning?" Graves asked from where he stood next to the window. He had obviously been the one to part the drapes.

"I can dress myself," Robert replied, suppressing the urge to groan. "Have hot water and the tub brought up to the bathing chamber, and bring a cup... no, make that *two* cups of chocolate for her ladyship."

The servant bowed. "Straight away, my lord."

"And close those damned drapes."

"Yes, my lord."

The room was suddenly shrouded in darkness before the butler rushed to the door and left the bedchamber.

Ivy tittered. "Told him, you did," she teased.

He turned over to face her and grinned, the expression making him appear years younger. "Except for a few days ago back in York, I don't think I've raised my voice like that with a servant in all the years I've been alive," he murmured.

"Well, now he knows never to open the drapes whilst you're still in bed," she chided.

"Damn right. I had plans for this morning," Robert said, struggling to swing his legs over the edge of the bed.

"Oh?"

"I was going to make love to you."

Ivy's eyes rounded. "Again?" she asked in shock.

He turned to regard her with an uncertain expression. "Would you... object?"

She lifted a bare shoulder. "Although I suppose I could manage, I am a bit sore," she replied. "Not in a bad way, though."

"I may not be able to walk," he countered, rising from the bed as he groaned. He staggered to the dressing room, his gait making it evident he found it difficult to walk.

Ivy tittered as she looked about for a robe of some sort. "Oh, dear. I shouldn't want to go into the mistress suite naked. I've nothing to wear but my gown from last night," she complained.

"I may be able to help," he said, his words muffled. He emerged from the dressing room with a banyan and brought it around to her side of the bed. He held it open for her as she stepped onto the carpet.

"Thank you," she whispered. She stood on tiptoes and kissed him on the cheek. "And thank you for ordering the chocolate and the bath, although I can't imagine why you think I need *two* cups of chocolate."

"One is for me," he replied. "As is the bath."

When her eyes widened and it appeared she was about to put voice to a protest, he grinned. "We can share," he suggested.

She tittered softly. "You're obviously not familiar with the bathtub," she replied dryly. "But I'm willing to try."

He chuckled as he made his way back to the dressing room. When he reappeared, he was wearing a velvet dressing robe.

"You look rather dashing in that," she remarked. "And warm," she added, tightening the lightweight banyan around her middle.

The sound of buckets of water being poured into a tub had

him peeking into the bathing chamber. "Ah, that was quick," he murmured.

"Cook is good about keeping cans of water warm when I'm in residence," Ivy said, joining him at the door. Once the servants had departed the bathing chamber, she hurried in and pulled some bath linens from a shelf. When she turned around, she found her husband standing over the tub, his arms crossed and his face displaying a curious expression. "What is it?"

He glanced up. "I'm not exactly sure which direction I should sit in this one," he remarked.

"I rather doubt it matters," she said.

"It does if we're both going in."

She placed the stack of bath linens on a nearby chair and doffed the banyan, tossing it on the back of the chair. "Well, we could sit back to back," she suggested.

"I rather doubt my knees will bend that much," he said, arching a graying brow. "Nor will I be able to get out when I'm done." He gingerly stepped into the water and gripped the edges so he could lower himself into the water. "It's not too hot," he said as he settled back. "Your turn."

Ivy was about to defer, but she saw how he had spread his knees to make room for her to sit between them. She gripped his outstretched hand and joined him, but before she lowered herself into the water, she asked, "Do I face you, or—oh!"

He had gripped his hands around her waist and had her back pressed against the front of his chest before she had a chance to finish her query, her bottom wedged between his thighs. She giggled as the water threatened to spill over the edge.

"Do you recall the first time we ever did this?" he asked when she was finally settled and her head lay against the front of one of his shoulders. Like his, her knees were bent and poked above the water line.

"The only time, you mean?" she asked in a quiet voice. "I think we flooded the entire second floor of Gladstone Hall," she said. "Before we could get it mopped up, the water seeped through the flooring into the room below—"

"Charity's bedchamber," Robert stated before he chuckled softly, his chest vibrating. "What a mess. Left a stain on the ceiling—"

"Which is why I arranged to have it painted by that Italian artist," she said with a titter. "I had always wanted a room done in the Italian style," she added wistfully. "With lots of marble and ornate trims and gilt mouldings."

"It was quite a project," he recalled.

"After it was finished, I remembered feeling so disappointed," Ivy went on. "All that time—the tassels and drops took months to be made—"

"Cost a year's profits from the earldom," Robert murmured.

"—the marble was delayed month after month—"

"Which cost another year's profit."

"—and by the time it was all finished, Charity had been staying in the guest bedchamber so long, she didn't even want to move back into it." Ivy angled her head to one side so she could look at him directly. "I don't recall you ever saying anything about it. Did you ever actually go into that room?"

"I might have peeked in a time or two," he admitted. "Weren't all those naked figures on the ceiling supposed to be cherubs?" he asked, glancing down to see that she had turned her head on his chest so she could glance up at him. Her coiffure from the day before, the pins no longer secure, was in danger of coming apart and spilling down the front of his chest and belly. He wouldn't have minded if it did. She looked like a siren from a Greek tale, as if he had captured her from the ocean's depths and brought her to the surface. He bent his head and dropped a kiss on her forehead.

She gave him a wistful grin. "Indeed. I didn't even give the subject matter a thought until Grace and Charity had their friends over one day, and I heard them all giggling," she said with a grin. "I think they were scandalized at the sight of all those naked men on the ceiling," she added. "Come to think of it, I think there were some naked women and centaurs, too."

"Still are," he said. At the sound of her gasp, he added, "I've never had that ceiling redone." He leaned down and placed another kiss on her forehead. "I recall finding Michael in there one day, lying on the floor and staring up at it."

"Oh?" Ivy gave a start. "I suppose I shouldn't be surprised. He loved art, especially Italian art—"

"He was staring at the naked women," Robert said, chuckling softly. "But I suppose I cannot blame him."

"The Kingdom of the Two Sicilies was his favorite during his Grand Tour," she reminded him.

"As I recall, Rome was your favorite on our wedding trip," he murmured. "All those naked men."

She gasped. "That is *not* why I liked Rome," she said, tittering softly. "It was all so beautiful. All the sights. All the art. It's why I had such high hopes for that damned bedchamber."

"It was not a failure, Ivy. It's actually quite a showpiece in an otherwise typical English manor house," he said. "In fact..."

When he didn't go on, Ivy furrowed a brow. "Go on," she prompted.

"If it had been on the first floor, I would have made it into the parlor, but since it was next door to the master suite, I might have had it turned into my private salon," he murmured. "Had a door added that leads into the master bedchamber so it's all sort of an apartment now."

Ivy blinked. "You're not joking," she said in awe.

"I am not. I rather like it. And so do the girls. They've both seen it since the remodel," he said. "Although I couldn't help but notice they still found it amusing. All that nakedness."

Tittering, Ivy lifted a shoulder. "I don't suppose it did any harm for the girls," she whispered.

"Probably better prepared them for their wedding nights," he murmured.

"Probably," she agreed, her voice sounding breathy. When one of his hands slid up her belly and over one breast, she inhaled sharply. Both of her nipples were pebbled in the cool air over the top of the water. She could feel his manhood stiffening against her hip, and she shifted to give it more room.

"I meant what I said about you coming to York after Christmastide," he murmured. "I don't want us to be apart any longer, Ivy."

She reached up and kissed him, the maneuver difficult given her position against the front of his body. "I guess a night of sleeping on it hasn't changed your mind?" she asked, swallowing hard.

He shook his head. "I miss you terribly when you're not with me," he whispered.

She took a deep breath. "And the ghosts?"

Dipping his head so his nose was buried in her hair, he shook it. The last of the hairpins gave up their hold, and her flame-colored locks spilled down past her shoulders. "I think you've managed to chase them all away."

Ivy relaxed into his hold and sighed contentedly. "Oh, Robert, I would make love to you right now if I thought there was enough room in this tub."

She let out a yelp when he suddenly straightened, lifted and turned her until she was facing him, her knees coming to rest on either side of his hips. Her breasts swelled and her nipples tightened in the cool air above the water as waves of her coppery hair threatened to hide them.

"Of all the sights in the world, this is my favorite," Robert growled. "*You* are my favorite. The very best gift I could have on Christmas."

"Oh," she breathed. "As are you, Robert," she whispered. "Happy Christmas."

When he leaned back again, she guided the tip of his manhood until it was at her entrance.

As she impaled herself on it, Robert's mouth covered one breast, his tongue laving over a taut nipple. Her gasp coincided with his first thrust. He answered with a groan and moved his mouth to her other breast, inciting frissons beneath her chilled skin, inciting heat in her core. Another thrust, and he was fully inside her, filling her with his manhood while his hands gripped her hips to guide them.

While waves of water splashed over the edge of the tub, she rode him until she felt the wash of warmth deep within and heard his growl of satisfaction.

They stayed half-emerged in the water for several moments, her head on his chest, the waves finally coming to rest.

"We're never getting out of this tub, are we?" she asked, nearly breathless.

He chuckled as he resettled his body against the back of the tub. "Never say never, my sweet. If there's a will, there's a way and all that rot."

It was a few minutes before he lifted her and she could get to her feet, another minute before she was safely out of the tub and could lend a hand to help him to stand, and another hour before they headed downstairs for a Christmas breakfast.

In the meantime, she made sure to mop up the water on the floor with as many bath linens as she could find.

CHAPTER 19
BOXING DAY

The following day, Tuesday, December 26, 1815
By the time Robert and Ivy awoke the day after Christmas, Ritchfield Park was nearly abandoned.

Earlier that morning, with the sun bright and the snow melting outside, Anne and Clara packed the remaining oranges and leftover Christmas food into boxes and crates for the servants to take to their families in Castleford.

Tom had driven Ivy's traveling coach, the housemaids and Clara riding inside while he shared the bench with Perkins. Meanwhile, Bobby had driven the gig with his wife and the rest of the servants. Once everyone was dropped off at their family's residences, it was Tom's plan to spend the afternoon shopping with Anne.

He had a ring to procure for their wedding.

Only the fire in the great hall burned continuously, the Yule log keeping the downstairs fairly warm. Upstairs, Ivy and Robert remained in bed in the master bedchamber, Robert occasionally venturing out of it to add another log or two to the fireplace there.

"You see. We can survive without servants," Ivy said, once he had climbed back into the bed, complaining of the cold, and had the quilts covering them.

"Only because the cook made us enough food to last the entire day," he argued, indicating the silver salver on which rested the remains of a minced pie, a loaf of bread, a hunk of cheese, apples, and a fruitcake. The water in the teapot had long ago cooled, but the wine bottle hadn't yet been touched.

"I can boil water," Ivy claimed. "Which means I can make boiled eggs and boiled potatoes and anything else that can be boiled."

He chuckled. "Ah, but can you grow your own food?" he challenged.

"It's true I don't garden, but I know how to shop. How to buy things from costermongers and at the market," she went on. "So we wouldn't starve."

"I am relieved to hear it," he said dryly.

Ivy tittered. "If you had stayed at Gladstone Hall for Christmas, wouldn't you be fox hunting today?"

He allowed a grunt. "Not if I could help it," he replied. "Which is why I'm rather glad it snowed so much."

"So... what would you be doing there? If you had stayed for Christmas?"

He inhaled and shrugged. "Reading, probably. Reviewing reports from the mines. Writing letters to the family," he ticked off. "And you?"

She considered the query. "I'm always here for Christmas," she reminded him. "So I usually sit by the fire in the great hall and work on an embroidery or read a novel while I drink tea and eat chocolates."

When Robert's eyes widened at the mention of chocolates, she tittered again. "Not *all* day. And just one or two pieces," she said. "Maybe three." When she saw how his brow arched, she sighed. "Oh, all right. Four or five."

He let out a guffaw before sobering. "From where do you even get this chocolate?" he asked, suspicious.

She tittered and lifted her shoulders, as if she was keeping a secret. "I bring it with me from London, of course."

His eyes widened. "Did you... did you bring any with you this year?"

She leaned over and surveyed the collection of food items on the salver. She plucked a chocolate from a small plate and handed it to him. "I didn't know you liked chocolate," she commented.

"There's probably a lot about me you don't know these days," he countered, biting into the dark confection. "Hmm. Rather rich," he murmured.

She leaned over and kissed the corner of his mouth, tasting some of the chocolate caught on his lips. "Hmm, indeed," she said.

He finished the chocolate and licked the remains from his thumb and forefinger. "You are certainly not shy about showing your affection these days," he remarked.

"Well, certainly not when chocolate is involved," she teased. She stared at him for a moment. "Does it bother you? When I show affection for you?"

He shook his head and once again licked the tips of the finger and thumb that had held the piece of chocolate. "It used to. When you did it in public," he admitted. "I used to be a stickler for propriety, but I think you knew that."

Ivy swallowed and stiffened. "Oh, I remember," she whispered, rolling her eyes.

"But if you kissed me today in the middle of King's Square in York, I wouldn't mind a bit," he claimed. "I would kiss you back, in fact. In front of God and everyone."

She sat up in the bed, a look of disbelief on her face. "Really?"

"It's true."

"What's happened, Robert? To change your mind?" She reached up and placed the back of her hand against his forehead. "You don't feel feverish."

He scoffed softly and reached for her hand with one of his. "You, I suppose," he said, bringing the hand to his lips to kiss the palm. When he didn't elaborate, she gripped her fingers around his hand and continued to stare at him. He finally added, "Christmas Eve, when we were waltzing. I knew all the servants were watching us—probably because they were waiting for us to go upstairs so they could go to bed."

"They weren't watching us dancing," she insisted.

"And they continued dancing long after we left."

"Oh, they were pretending they weren't," he said with a *huff*, "but I could feel their gaze on us. Yesterday, too, when we were having Christmas dinner."

"That's because there were only a few couples dancing the waltz," she murmured. "Who else were they going to watch?"

"Besides that," he insisted. "It's as if they were waiting with bated breath to see if we were going to do something scandalous."

She relaxed into the pillows behind her and purred. "So I suppose it was a good thing that I did kiss you," she whispered.

He nodded. "I kissed you as well," he reminded her. "But I waited until the waltz was done," he added. "Until I could get us under the kissing bough."

Attempting to suppress a grin, Ivy tittered. "It was a bit awkward trying to kiss you whilst we danced, but I couldn't help myself," she said.

"The servants didn't seem to mind a bit," he said.

"I thought Graves was going to suffer apoplexy."

"I think he did," Robert remarked before he chuckled.

She grinned and lifted a bare shoulder. "So... now that I know you like chocolate and you're fine with being kissed in public, what else has changed about you in the last decade that I might not know about?"

Robert arched a brow. "Well, we have another ten days before Twelfth Night and when we leave for York for you to discover," he murmured.

Ivy's eyes darkened. "Is that some sort of challenge?" she asked, suspicion evident in her voice.

He chuckled. "Maybe."

She narrowed her eyes. "Challenge accepted."

They remained in bed the rest of the day.

CHAPTER 20
EPILOGUE

A few months later, York

On a rare sunny morning outside the ancient doors of Holy Trinity Micklegate church in York, the Lord and Lady Ritchfield congratulated Mr. and Mrs. Walker on their nuptials. The two had signed the marriage certificate as witnesses only a few minutes earlier, the stained glass windows on the east side of the building casting them in blue, green, red, and yellow light.

"Are you sure you won't join us for the ride back to Gladstone Park?" Tom asked, indicating the curricle parked in front of the second oldest church in York. The servants had decorated the equipage for the wedding, with old shoes tied at the end of streamers so they would drag on the street behind the curricle.

Ivy and Robert exchanged quick glances. "This is your day," the earl said. "Cook should have your wedding breakfast ready when you arrive, and the entire staff knows they have the rest of the day off to help you celebrate," he added.

"Oh, but do save some cake for us," Ivy said. "I look forward to having some with tea later today."

"Of course we will," Anne assured her. "And thank you again for the gown. It's far nicer than my Sunday best," she added, holding out the blush-colored silk skirt Ivy had gifted her the week before. Anne had discovered it in one of the three trunks that had arrived from London on the mail coach the month before.

"I'm so glad you could wear it. It hasn't fit me in an age, so I was surprised when Watkins sent it up with my other gowns," Ivy replied. In truth, the color never suited her complexion nor her hair color. On her lady's maid, it was the perfect gown for a wedding.

"My lord, if I'm not to drive you, how will you get back to Gladstone Hall?" Tom asked with concern.

"Walk, probably," Robert replied. "If we grow tired, there is always a hackney about."

"We're going to take advantage of this lovely day to get some air," Ivy said. "And I won't require your services until tomorrow morning," she added, turning her attention back to her lady's maid.

"*Late* tomorrow morning," Robert put in, arching a teasing brow. He held out his right hand to Tom. "Keep her happy," he said as he shook hands with the driver.

"It's my every intention, my lord."

Robert and Ivy watched as the two servants climbed into the curricle, Tom taking up the reins to drive the single white horse past Micklegate Bar and the walls surrounding the city of York.

Ivy waved as the equipage merged into traffic and then she and the earl regarded one another a moment with grins.

"Acting as their witness has meant you have missed your regular visit to the boxing saloon this morning," she remarked. "Do you wish to go now?" she asked, waving in the general direction of the city.

Robert shook his head. "I haven't been for several weeks."

Blinking, Ivy placed a hand on his proffered arm. "What? But I thought—"

"I don't go because I haven't felt the need to punch anything since Christmas," he said proudly, leading them toward the River Ouse. "Thanks to you."

Ivy inhaled softly. Although she had worried he might regret inviting her to stay with him in York, they had settled into a comfortable and satisfying life at Gladstone Hall. "So... where have you been going every Saturday morning whilst I've been having breakfast?" she asked.

He chuckled softly. "Taking a long walk is all," he said, his gaze darting down to the water as they crossed the bridge.

"Where do you go?"

He shrugged. "Usually into town. Sometimes I walk the walls, and sometimes I stop for a bite of chocolate, or I find a costermonger selling oranges," he said with a shrug.

"So that's where the chocolate's been coming from," she murmured. Every so often, a piece of it would be included with her breakfast, and she had no idea why since she had never included it on the menu.

"I do love watching you eat it," he said, grinning as they made their way on High Ousegate Street.

She returned her grin, sure her face was red from hearing his comment. "I do wish it had been warmer today," she remarked.

"Well, if it's any consolation, the cool weather has certainly helped the earldom's profits," he said. "Michael and I reviewed this past year's ledgers, and I must say, I am quite happy with what he's done by way of improvements. He's bought lamps which use a special battery from the Kingdom of the Two Sicilies, and he's changed the schedules so the miners are working fewer hours."

"For less pay?" she asked, her brows furrowed.

"No. Same pay, because for some reason, their quotas

remain the same and they still meet them," he replied, a brow furrowed as if he was still trying to sort how that could be.

"I would call that an incentive," she commented. "And it sounds as if it's working."

He grunted his agreement as he led them onto Pavement Street.

"I am so glad Michael has taken an interest in running the business of the earldom," she remarked. "But it's a shame it requires him to live in Wakefield."

"He doesn't mind," Robert said. "He has his own bedchamber in the townhouse there, and so will Charles once he's back on British shores."

Ivy's eyes widened. "Charles is going to live in Wakefield?" When she had first arrived at Gladstone Hall in January, word came from their youngest son that he would be returning from his Grand Tour sometime that summer.

"According to his latest letter, which I received this morning, yes," Robert said. He knew Ivy would react with dismay and quickly patted the gloved hand on his arm. "I would have had you read it after I did, but you were quite busy with your lady's maid," he reminded her. "Acting as *her* lady's maid," he chided.

Ivy tittered. "I could not help it. She always does such beautiful work on my hair, so it was only fair I do a coiffure for her on her wedding day," she argued.

"You did a beautiful job, which has me wondering why you need her," he teased.

She gasped. "I cannot do my own like that," she argued. "I would require three hands and a mirror in the front and back." She glanced up at him. "And it would take me far too long."

He nodded his understanding as he turned them north onto Colliergate.

"So… what other news from Charles?" she asked, remembering they had been discussing his letter.

"He has spent the past few weeks living in his sister's household in Rome, which has him claiming he is a most excellent uncle but not of a mind to become a father himself," Robert remarked, his brows arched in preparation for hearing her disappointment.

"He's far too young to wed," she said.

Robert chuckled. "That was not what I was expecting you to say," he commented.

Ivy aimed a happy grin in his direction. "Charles will be sorry to have left the warmth of the Mediterranean when he gets here," she said on a sigh. "But it will be so good to have him living close to us again."

Robert murmured his agreement. "Speaking of the Mediterranean, I was thinking we might pay a call on Grace and her husband." He waited for his wife's reaction, curious how she would respond.

"You mean after she returns from Rome, or…?" Her eyes rounded as she suddenly stopped and turned to face him. "… or that we're to go *there*?"

Robert chuckled, dropping his head so the rim of his hat touched hers. "Since Michael can see to the mines in my absence, I thought it past time we take a holiday," he said.

"But… but what about Parliament? We're supposed to leave for London next week," she reminded him as they resumed their walk. "Easter is in a fortnight."

"When the session is over. In June, I am hoping."

"Oh, that will be lovely," she replied in awe.

"Normally, I wouldn't even think of going to Rome or Greece in the summer, but—"

"It's been so cold here," she finished for him. Her eyes rounded at realizing what he had said. "Greece, too?"

"Indeed," he replied with a chuckle, noting they had

reached King's Square. He was about to say more, but Ivy was suddenly on tiptoes, a hand behind his neck pulling his head down so she could kiss him.

And kiss him she did, her enthusiasm nearly sending his top hat from his head.

Ivy didn't let go of him right away, either, but continued to kiss him, slipping her tongue betwixt his lips and tasting him until she had no choice but to come up for air.

Finally released from the kiss, Robert blinked several times. He was well aware there were a few couples staring at them in shock. A woman passed them on the pavement, making a sound of disgust as she did so, although she slowed her pace and turned around to continue watching them. A few children intrigued enough to stop their play with a rubber ball gawked until the ball threatened to roll away toward Petergate, and they were forced to race after it.

He didn't mind, though. He had been warned during their stay at Ritchfield Park that something like this could happen.

He rather hoped it would.

"You minx," he said with a huge grin, loving how her face displayed a blush and her lips appeared bright pink under the midday sun. "I am yours, Ivy. Always have been. For now and the rest of my life."

Ivy placed her arm on his and turned to resume their walk. "Just you wait until we're in Rome," she warned happily.

Robert guffawed. "Perhaps we won't go to London at all this Season," he murmured, not expecting her to kiss him again.

The woman who stared at them fainted, and the rubber ball disappeared into a thicket of ivy.

AUTHOR NOTES

Hanging of the greens

The Christmas tradition of the "hanging of the greens" has been around for centuries. Sprays, garlands, wreaths, and branches from evergreen trees such as pine, holly, fir, and laurel have decorated homes at Christmas time since the days of Martin Luther in the early 1500s. In England, the greenery wasn't brought into the house until the day of Christmas Eve and remained until Epiphany when it was burned lest it bring bad luck to the house.

The winter of 1815

Several volcanic eruptions took place between 1812 and 1815 and resulted in what is sometimes called a "volcanic winter" across Northern Europe and North America. England experienced one of its worst winters and coldest summers on record (1816 is referred to as *The Year of No Summer*). Excessive rain (every day of June) led to massive crop failures. The high levels of tephra in the atmosphere caused a haze to hang over the sky for several years, resulting in brilliant sunsets. Artist J.M.W. Turner captured the effect in many of his paintings.

Your Invitation!

Do you crave historical romance filled with passion and red-hot chemistry?

Come join me and my author friends in the Facebook group, Historical Harlots, for exclusive giveaways, chats with amazing HistRom authors, raunchy shenanigans, and more! https://www.facebook.com/groups/2102138599813601

ABOUT THE AUTHOR

A self-described nerd and lover of science, Linda Rae spent many years as a published technical writer specializing in 3D graphics workstations, software and 3D animation (her movie credits include SHREK and SHREK 2). Mythology, immortality, and ancient Greece have been lifelong interests.

A fan of action-adventure movies, she can frequently be found at the local cinema. Although she no longer has any tropical fish, she does follow the San Jose Sharks. She makes her home in Cody, Wyoming.

For more information:
www.lindaraesande.com
Sign up for Linda Rae's newsletter:
Regency Romance with a Twist

www.ingramcontent.com/pod-product-compliance
Lightning Source LLC
Chambersburg PA
CBHW030859200726
48289CB00003B/821